# AUTUMN TIDES

MEREDITH SUMMERS

"Hard to believe the inn has four guests even in the offseason," Jane said, sharing a contented smile with her sister, Andie.

Earlier that year, when their mother had fallen ill, Jane had doubted her ability to manage the family inn, Tides. Now, the inn was thriving, a testament to her perseverance.

Andie looked into the dining room, where four women were enjoying breakfast. "They seem like they're having a good time."

"They are," Jane affirmed. She caught a glimpse of the ocean beyond, a serene backdrop that never grew old. "They grew up here, I guess, and were best friends. Now, they come back for Prelude every year to catch up."

"That's nice." Andie smiled in at the ladies. "Do you need any help with things here?"

Jane shook her head. "No, I've got Brenda in the kitchen and Liz up front. You have your own business to tend to."

"I don't mind helping out. I did just get in some interesting items from an estate sale that I'm dying to pick through, though. Found some old trunks up in an attic."

Jane could see the excited gleam in her sister's eye. Andie used to be an antique curator at a high-end auction house but had come back home when their mom got sick. Now she had her own antique store right in town. "Then you should get to it. Could be a treasure in there."

Andie laughed and hugged Jane. "Let's hope! Give me a shout if you need anything."

Jane watched her sister leave and then picked up the coffee carafe and entered the dining room. The aroma of fresh coffee mingled with the scent of bacon and eggs. "Would anyone like a top-off?"

Four heads turned, their faces breaking into smiles. Susan, her short gray bob impeccably styled, held out her cup with manicured fingers. "Oh, yes, dear, please," she said.

As Jane went around refilling mugs, Betty's eyes

met hers. "How is your mother, Addie? We remember she was such a gracious hostess. A true gem of Lobster Bay."

Jane felt her chest tighten briefly but masked it with a smile. "She's well. Thank you for asking. She's in a memory-care unit at an assisted living facility. She's comfortable and well taken care of."

"Oh, I'm so sorry to hear about the memory care," Susan said, sympathy filling her eyes. "But it's good she's in a safe place."

"Thank you." Jane nodded, eager to lift the mood. "So, you all grew up here in town? I bet it hasn't changed much."

The four of them laughed.

"It really hasn't," said Carol, tall and elegant with striking snow-white hair. "That's a good thing. The town is charming. I grew up over on Willow Street, and there are a few new houses but not much else different."

Susan, wearing a blouse that spoke of her penchant for meticulous order, picked up the thread. "And I was on Harbor Lane. Still pretty much the same there."

Betty's eyes were a soft green, almost the color of sea foam, framed by wavy salt-and-pepper hair. She wore a comfortable, oversized knit sweater and a chunky silver charm bracelet on her right wrist. "I grew up on Elm Street. It was a lovely place until...." Her voice trailed off, and her eyes grew sad.

Carol reached over and patted her hand.

Jane stood there awkwardly until Betty sighed and looked up. "My sister, Heidi, died when she was seventeen. Car accident. I was only fifteen and adored her. I never got to say goodbye. We had such a happy life in that house until then."

"I'm so sorry." Jane's heart ached for Betty.

Betty waved her hand dismissively and smiled. "Well, that was long ago, and I've come to terms. Still, I do always hope she'll give me some sort of sign when I'm back here."

"Lobster Bay has its own way of sending signs. Who knows? Maybe this visit will be special."

"I hope so," Betty said then deftly changed the subject. "Anyway, we've all had quite varied careers since then. I went into marine biology."

"And I became a stewardess—flew all over the world!" Carol said, her voice tinged with nostalgia.

"That sounds amazing," Jane said.

"I didn't do anything quite so exciting. I became an accountant," Susan added, a playful glint in her eyes. "Someone had to make sense of the numbers."

"Very true," Jane nodded.

Margie, vibrant in a flowy boho skirt and tank top that showcased her assortment of arm tattoos, waved a hand adorned with chunky rings. "I became a fashion designer."

"That's a diverse set of careers," Jane marveled.

"We like to keep things interesting." Margie winked, her bangles jingling with the motion. "These days, our competition has shifted to buying the best gifts for our grandchildren. We're hoping to pick up some unique items here in town."

"Oh, how lovely!"

"It's our own version of *The Price Is Right*," Carol joked.

"I think you'll find exactly what you want."

Jane's phone chirped with an incoming text, and she left the ladies to their conversation. Pulling the phone out of her apron, she saw it was from one of her best friends, Maxi.

---

SOS! *Art Gallery Chaos! HELP!*

# CHAPTER TWO

Jane pushed open the gallery door, stepping into an airy space that felt like a war zone rather than the sanctuary of art it usually was. The room was generous in size, its floor-to-ceiling windows and overhead skylights usually offering an inviting luminescence. White walls, normally the quiet backdrop for vibrant art, today seemed to amplify the tension in the room. At opposite ends stood two artists, each guarding their exhibit as if it were a fortress. Both wore expressions sharp enough to etch glass. Maxi, her long white hair twisted into a messy bun, was caught in the crossfire, standing between them. Her arms moved erratically, punctuating the air as she attempted—unsuccessfully, it appeared—to play mediator.

"What on earth is going on?" Jane said, slipping in next to Maxi.

Maxi's expression was a mix of relief and exasperation. "Oh, thank heavens you're here! Meet Gerard, a fine sculptor specializing in blending Native American art with digital installations. And this is Priya, an incredible painter who merges classical Renaissance techniques with Bollywood themes."

Jane took in the exhibits. Gerard's space was filled with intricate sculptures that incorporated digital elements—like a totem pole that transformed into a virtual waterfall via a projection. On Priya's side, richly colored canvases showcased sumptuous Renaissance-styled portraits in saris and turbans, adorned with flashy Bollywood jewelry.

"The problem," Maxi sighed, "is that they both want the centerpiece spot for their exhibit, and neither will budge."

"I was here first," Gerard grumbled, arms crossed. "My installation needs the central space for the digital projections to work correctly."

"And I should have the central spot," Priya retorted, "because the lighting there will highlight the jewel tones in my paintings!"

Jane looked at Maxi. "They both have valid points. But why not try to see this as an opportunity?"

"An opportunity for what?" Maxi asked, clearly at her wits' end.

"Working together maybe?" Jane threw a hopeful look at the two artists.

Gerard threw up his hands. "That's it! I will not share my space with her primitive pieces!"

Priya shot back, "Primitive? At least my art has soul, not like your superficial pop art!"

"I'm leaving, Maxi. Make your choice," Gerard huffed.

"And I'm taking my work with me," Priya declared.

"In that case, I'm leaving first!" Gerard said, marching toward the door.

"No, I am!" Priya insisted, quickening her pace to beat him to it.

The two artists arrived at the gallery's entrance simultaneously, both hands reaching for the doorknob. They glared at each other, stuck in a comedic deadlock, each refusing to let go. Finally, they pulled the door open and stormed out, shoulders bumping, both muttering under their breath.

Maxi sighed, brushing a stray lock of white hair from her forehead. "Well, that went well," she said, the sarcasm dripping from each word.

Claire burst into the gallery, her eyes darting from

the departing artists to Maxi and Jane. "I got your emergency text. What on earth is going on here?"

Maxi ran a hand over her messy white bun, looking utterly defeated. "Just a minor catastrophe. Those two artists couldn't agree on exhibit space, and now they've both stormed off, threatening to pull their work."

"Oh no!" Claire adjusted her auburn curls as she glanced back out the window.

Maxi sighed and flopped down onto a white cement cube that was supposed to hold a sculpture. "Those are the only two artists that I could find who had work that included a holiday theme with a cultural twist. Chandler is not going to be happy that I messed up my first time hosting a gallery event."

"Don't worry. We can fix this. Any chance we can get them back?" Claire asked.

Maxi shrugged, "I doubt it. Their egos are as big as their talent."

Claire rolled her eyes. "Tell me about it. It's not just artists, either. Restaurant owners too."

"What do you mean?" Jane asked.

Claire sighed, taking a seat next to Maxi. "Coordinating the menu for Taste of the Town is like trying to organize a herd of cats. Everyone wants their dish to shine, but nobody wants to overlap flavors or types of cuisine. There's an unspoken rivalry among some of the restaurant owners—you can cut the tension with a knife. Or a fork, depending on the dish."

Jane grinned mischievously. "Ah, rivalry among cooks. But I bet you and Rob are on the same page."

Claire's cheeks flushed a rosy hue. Earlier in the year, she'd started dating Rob Bradford, who owned the bread store across the street from Sandcastles. "Rob and I are perfectly in sync, thank you very much."

"And what's going on with Beach Bones? Did you talk to Sandee?" Jane queried, glancing between Maxi and Claire. Claire had started a line of homemade dog biscuits in her bakery and named the line Beach Bones. Unfortunately, she'd discovered someone else was using the name. Even worse, it was her ex-husband's new trophy wife, Sandee.

Claire shook her head, worry lines etching her forehead. "I don't know what to do. I probably should just pick another name."

Maxi's eyes flared with indignation. "She can't do that! That's your brand, your hard work. You can't let her take that too, Claire."

"So you haven't talked to her about it?" Jane asked.

Claire grimaced. "No, not yet. I've been avoiding

the confrontation. It's complicated, you know? Tammi said I might be making too much of it."

Tammi was Claire's grown daughter who was off at college. Jane wasn't exactly sure where Tammi stood on the subject of Sandee. Tammi had only been a teen when the divorce had occurred. Claire had tried to shield her from the nastiness and never spoke badly of Peter because he was Tammi's dad.

"Tammi might not see things the way we do," Jane said.

Maxi huffed, "Well, you could always try to outsell her. I've seen Sandee's business ventures; she has the attention span of a goldfish. She'll lose interest and move on to the next shiny object soon enough."

"I don't know, Maxi. It's a risky strategy. What if she doesn't give up? What if she makes it her mission to dominate the dog biscuit market? I don't really want any drama."

Jane sighed. "It sounds like you have some tough decisions to make, Claire. But remember, you're not alone. We're here to support you, just like we're all here to help Maxi with her gallery crisis."

"Speaking of which," Maxi interjected, "we still need to figure out what to do about these empty walls."

"Sounds like we need a girls' night out." Jane wiggled her brows.

"Great idea!" Maxi pulled up the calendar on her phone. "We had a couples' night last week, so the guys won't feel left out. How about tomorrow night?"

"Sounds good to me." Jane pulled out her phone. "I'll send a text to Andie. Should we plan for six at Barnacle Billy's?"

# CHAPTER THREE

A ndie's phone pinged with a text. It was Jane wanting to know if she was free for a girls' night out on Thursday. Of course she was!

Warmth bloomed in her chest at the invitation. She hadn't always been this close with her sister; in fact, there had been a time when they'd only spoken on holidays. Moving back to Lobster Bay was the best decision Andie had ever made, and now her life was perfect. She had her friends and even had reconnected with the love of her life, Shane Flannery.

She loved that she, Jane, Maxi, and Claire had formed a friendship bond. She hadn't had close friends when she'd lived in the city, and she cherished their frequent get-togethers. Usually, they met at Sandcastles for coffee a few times a week. In the summer, they liked to go to Splash after work since it was right on the beach, but it was too cold for that now. So they'd moved to Barnacle Billy's in Perkins Cove, where they could watch the boats in the cove.

Her fingers tapped out a jubilant "Yes!" on the screen before returning her phone to the counter and picking up the feather duster she'd been using to dust off the antiques in her store.

Amid the charm of weathered cabinets and glass-fronted display cases, Andie's antique store was a treasure trove of history and beauty. From vintage jewelry to midcentury furniture, the store was a testament to Andie's keen eye for unique finds. The polished hardwood floors gave off a warm, inviting glow, and the overhead track lighting was strategically aimed to showcase the best pieces. Antique chandeliers hung from the ceiling, illuminating the space with a soft, welcoming light.

Customers often felt like they were stepping back in time, and today was no different. A few were scattered throughout the store, their eyes wide with curiosity as they rifled through crates of vinyl records or examined ornate picture frames. A faint scent of aged wood and polish filled the air, adding to the nostalgia.

A customer approached the register, holding a delicately painted vase adorned with intricate floral patterns and a crackled glaze. It was one of Andie's favorite pieces, and she had almost hesitated to sell it.

"Isn't this just beautiful?" the customer remarked, setting the vase on the counter.

"It is," Andie agreed, her eyes meeting the customer's as she began wrapping the vase carefully in protective tissue. "It's a special piece—nineteenth-century French porcelain. You have excellent taste."

The customer beamed, clearly pleased with her find. Andie processed the payment, handed over the bag containing the vase, and bid her customer a cheerful goodbye.

Andie picked up the duster again and started cleaning an antique slag glass lamp that sat atop a vintage writing desk. The lamp's intricate metalwork and colorful, marbled glass had caught her eye at an estate sale months ago. As she moved the duster in gentle circles, her eyes wandered to a pair of old trunks tucked away in the corner of the store.

Those trunks had come from the attic of a stately home, hidden so well among cobwebs and old furniture that most people had missed them. Andie had only had the chance for a cursory look inside each, but the initial peek had revealed a tantalizing glimpse of

17

old books, tarnished jewelry, and fabric that might've been clothing or linens from decades—maybe even centuries—past.

The customer who had been browsing in the back had made her way out the door, and finally, Andie was alone in the store.

"No time like the present," she thought, setting aside the duster and hurrying over to the trunks.

With a sense of expectation tingling at the back of her mind, she pulled one of the trunks closer to a cushioned chair meant for customers to take a load off while contemplating a potential purchase. She unbuckled the rusted latch, its creaking sound accompanied by a puff of dust that spoke of long-kept secrets.

As the lid swung open, a musty but not unpleasant odor wafted up—a mixture of aged leather, wood, and the indefinable scent of old things long stored away. It felt as if she was about to open a time capsule. Her fingers tingled with anticipation as she considered the untold stories that might be hidden within.

Andie could hardly wait to explore the contents. As she began to carefully lift out the topmost items—a couple of old books and what appeared to be a hand-embroidered shawl—she felt a rush of excitement.

Digging deeper into the trunk, Andie uncovered a

porcelain figurine of a ballerina, one arm gracefully stretched above her head, though her tutu was chipped at the edges. Next, she found a small tin box filled with vintage postcards, the faded images capturing long-gone landscapes and landmarks.

But as she moved these items aside, she noticed something incongruous with the other treasures. Tossed haphazardly at the bottom were what appeared to be Christmas decorations. Garland, plastic mistletoe. Some ornaments had been placed there without much care, and sadly, a few were smashed, their shattered pieces intermingling with strands of tarnished tinsel.

And there, partially buried by a broken ornament and a sprig of artificial mistletoe, was a sad little present. It was still wrapped in yellowing paper that must've once been vibrant and cheerful. A frayed ribbon barely held its bow together. A tiny tag dangled from it, the ink faded but still legible. It read, "To Urchin."

Urchin? Was that a nickname? Andie couldn't help but wonder who it was and why this gift had never found its way into their hands. A sense of melancholy washed over her as she considered the countless possible stories behind this unopened gift.

As she looked at the tag, she felt an inexplicable connection to its intended recipient, a responsibility to try to find out who it belonged to. And she knew exactly who she could ask to help.

## CHAPTER FOUR

Jane returned to Tides after talking Maxi down off the ledge. Cooper, her golden Lab, bounded into the foyer, his tail wagging energetically. Jane bent down to give him a quick scratch behind the ears. "Hey, Coop. Miss me?"

Cooper's wagging tail seemed to say "Always" as he circled her legs before settling down, eyeing the decorations on the counter with canine curiosity.

As she straightened up, Liz Weston looked up from the front desk and greeted her with a smile. "You're just in time. Olga Svenson dropped off some Norwegian Christmas decorations that she made herself. She thought they'd be perfect for the Prelude."

Jane's eyes widened as she approached the collection spread out on the counter. Traditional straw ornaments, delicately carved wooden figures, and intricately woven heart-shaped baskets caught her eye. A small tomte, a mythological creature resembling a gnome, sat in a corner, its red cap tilted just so.

"Olga really outdid herself, didn't she?" Jane beamed, clearly pleased with the array.

"She likes to keep busy," Liz agreed, casting a glance at Cooper, who seemed intrigued by the straw ornaments.

"I'll say."

"Her children keep pressing her to move to assisted living, you know." Liz shook her head. "She's ninety-five and can craft better than anyone I know. Not to mention she still manages to walk three times a day. She's more than capable of living on her own."

"I couldn't agree more." Jane nodded, picking up one of the straw ornaments and twirling it gently between her fingers and looking around to pick out a place to put it. "I think the baskets could go over here, and maybe we could hang the paper chains on the window." Jane stopped and narrowed her gaze at the window in the foyer, where the top trim seemed to be a bit loose. "Guess I'll need to call Sally to fix that first."

There was always something to repair in these old houses, and Sally was the local handywoman who Jane practically had on speed dial.

Jane looked up from her conversation with Liz to see Susan, Betty, Carol, and Margie coming in the front door, arms loaded with shopping bags from their early outing.

Cooper bounded over to the ladies.

"Cooper!" Carol cooed, dropping her bags to hug the exuberant dog.

"He's a sweetheart, isn't he?" Jane said, beaming as Cooper wagged his tail furiously, clearly enjoying the attention.

"We're going upstairs to change," Betty announced after all four of them had fawned over the dog. "We want to walk the Marginal Way. We always loved it as kids, and it's something of a tradition for us, even if it's a bit chilly right now."

"We've got our new Lobster Bay sweatshirts," Susan added, lifting a bag as proof.

"Sounds like a lovely plan," Jane said.

Margie caught sight of the festive setup. "Oh my, these Norwegian decorations are absolutely adorable!"

"Thank you! They're courtesy of our neighbor, Olga Svenson. She's in her nineties and still as crafty as ever," Liz chimed in.

"Aww, how sweet," Susan said.

"As a little evening treat, would you ladies like to

have a glass of wine in the living room later? The view of the ocean is quite spectacular," Jane offered.

"That sounds heavenly," Carol said. "A glass of wine would be perfect."

"How about I set out some cheese and crackers as well?" Jane suggested.

"Oh, you're a gem, Jane. That would be fantastic," Betty said, her eyes twinkling.

Carol turned to Cooper. "We'll even bring a treat for you. We'll pick up some Beach Bones from Sandcastles." Carol glanced up at Jane. "If that's okay with you?"

Jane smiled. "Of course. He loves them."

The ladies went upstairs, and Jane and Liz continued finding places for the Norwegian Christmas decorations, but now Jane's mind was on Beach Bones and Claire's situation with Sandee. With both Claire and Maxi having some drama, Jane was glad things were calm for her. Still, she couldn't wait for girls' night out so that she could try to help her friends solve their problems.

# CHAPTER FIVE

C laire filled in the last restaurant assignment in the Taste of the Town event sheet. There, that should do it! She'd somehow managed to wrangle the other town restaurateurs into some sort of schedule and series of foods that would be fun for visitors and not too repetitive.

Putting the pencil behind her ear, she sighed, stretched her arms, and looked over the busy café. Sandcastles Bakery was doing well, filled with aroma of freshly baked pastries and the chatter of satisfied customers. Her signature sandcastle-shaped cakes sat proudly in the display case, enticing everyone who walked by.

When she glanced across the street, her eyes met Rob's, who was standing in the window of Bradford

25

Breads. He gave her a warm wave, which she happily returned, feeling a surge of warmth and affection.

Turning her attention back to the café, she saw Hailey, her ever-efficient assistant, topping off coffees for the customers. Among them were Bert and Harry, their newly adopted dog tied up outside the café. Claire smiled; they looked content. Then there were Sam and Bunny, snuggled in a cozy corner booth. It warmed Claire's heart to see them so smitten in their later years. Sam's dog, Dooley, was outside, munching on one of Claire's popular Beach Bones dog treats.

The thought of Beach Bones made her grimace. She still needed to confront Sandee about the whole name-stealing issue.

As if conjured by her thoughts, the door swung open, and in walked Sandee, a slim, young blonde dressed in high heels and an outfit that screamed high-maintenance. There was no avoiding her now. Sandee was headed straight for the counter.

Claire took a deep breath, preparing for the inevitable confrontation. The warm and fuzzy feeling from waving at Rob was now replaced by a knot of tension. But it had to be done. She braced herself and greeted Sandee with a practiced smile. "Hi, Sandee. What can I get for you today?"

Sandee's eyes darted over to the Beach Bones

display before settling back on Claire. "We need to talk," she said, her voice tinged with a mixture of accusation and vulnerability.

"About the Beach Bones?" Claire guessed, feeling her own defenses rise.

"Exactly," Sandee replied, crossing her arms. "Why would you steal my product name? Is this some sort of payback for me marrying Pete?"

Claire sighed, her eyes narrowing slightly. "Hardly, Sandee. First of all, I had no idea you had a dog biscuit company named Beach Bones. And for all I know, you could have stolen the name from me."

At Claire's words, a flicker of hurt crossed Sandee's eyes. For a moment, Claire saw a glimpse of something more complex behind Sandee's polished exterior. Perhaps it was vulnerability or even a tinge of regret.

"So you didn't do this intentionally?" Sandee finally asked, her voice softer than before.

"Of course not," Claire responded, her own voice softening as well.

"Then you won't mind changing the name," Sandee said, her voice resuming its earlier edge.

The suggestion rankled Claire. It would be just like Sandee to expect Claire to change to accommodate her. "Actually, I think you should be the one to change the name. I've built up my bakery, and Beach Bones has already been integrated into my brand."

Sandee's face flushed a shade of pink that clashed with her carefully chosen lipstick. "Why should I change? You already have this whole bakery, clients, a reputation. I'm just starting to build something for myself. I should be the one to keep the name!"

"Why? I don't think it matters who has what. It matters who used it first!" Claire retorted, her own arms crossing in a gesture that mirrored Sandee's defensive stance.

"Right, and I was the one who used it first."

Claire's eyes narrowed. "Can you prove that?"

Sandee huffed and gnawed her bottom lip. Finally, she said, "Fine, have it your way. But this isn't over."

With that, Sandee turned sharply and walked toward the door, her high heels clicking against the wooden floor like tiny gavels declaring a hung jury. Just as she reached the doorway, she nearly collided with Andie, who was walking in.

"Watch where you're going!" Sandee snapped, not breaking stride as she pushed through the door. She left Andie looking puzzled and Claire sighing in a mixture of relief and trepidation.

"I see you and Sandee finally talked about Beach

Bones." Andie glanced back at Sandee's retreating form.

Claire rolled her eyes. "Yep, and she won't budge."

"And I hope you won't, either."

"Not after the way she was acting, I won't." Claire waved her hand dismissively. "But anyway, at least that's over with now. Now, what can I get you? We have a new pastry that I'm going to feature at Taste of the Town: a caramel apple croissant, perfect for autumn. Want to give it a try?"

Andie's eyes lit up. "That sounds divine. I'll have one of those and a coffee, please."

"Coming right up," Claire said, signaling to Hailey, her helper, who began preparing the coffee.

"So, what brings you here today?" Claire continued, handing Andie the flaky, warm croissant on a delicate plate.

"Actually, I came to see Bunny and Sam," Andie said, taking the croissant and coffee. "I have a little mystery they might be able to help me with."

Claire's left brow shot up. "Do tell."

Andie leaned in, her voice dropping to a conspiratorial whisper. "Well, you know I've been going through those old trunks I found at the estate sale, right? I found some Christmas stuff hastily thrown in there and one sad little present, still wrapped."

"Aww, that is sad. So you're trying to track down the recipient?"

"That's right. Can't think of anyone better than Sam and Bunny to help." With that, Andie picked up her coffee, gave Claire a friendly wave, and headed toward the corner table, where Sam and Bunny were bent over a crossword puzzle, oblivious to the drama that had just unfolded at the counter.

---

SANDEE HURRIED DOWN THE STREET, her high heels clicking rapidly against the pavement. She clenched her designer handbag tightly, trying to keep her composure until she was out of sight. Her eyes brimmed with tears she didn't want Claire or Andie or anyone else in that café to see. As soon as she rounded the corner, she took a deep breath, her hand pressed against her chest.

"Why does everything have to be so complicated?" she muttered to herself.

She had genuinely thought Beach Bones was a brilliant name for her new line of dog treats. It was a cute play on words, and she never dreamed it would overlap with anything Claire was doing. The last thing she wanted was to be perceived as the town villain, especially after the whole ordeal with Peter.

"Peter," she muttered under her breath, her grip tightening around her bag. The name alone churned her stomach. Sandee felt misunderstood by the community, and much of it tied back to him.

Everyone thought she was a home-wrecker, the younger woman who had snatched up a married man. But they didn't know the full story. Peter had told her he was separated when they met, and she had naively believed him. Only later did she discover the reality of the situation, leaving her feeling foolish and used.

Sandee sighed, brushing a stray tear from her cheek. She needed to make things right, but she didn't know how. Everyone seemed to be on Claire's side and rightly so.

As she walked away, her mind raced with thoughts of how to mend her tarnished reputation, starting with the Beach Bones debacle. She should have let Claire use the name, but for some reason, her pride had taken over. Giving up that name seemed like giving up the one thing she had. Perhaps there was a way to resolve this without lawyers and public drama. But for now, she'd retreat, pull herself together, and think of a new strategy.

Sandee spotted a medium-sized black-and-white

dog tethered to a lamppost, its owner inside the Lobster Bay gift store. The dog's tail wagged as she approached. Kneeling, she extended her hand, letting the dog sniff her before she stroked its head. The simple, unconditional affection from the animal lifted her spirits, even if just a little.

"I wish people were as easy to understand as animals are," she said softly to the dog, scratching it behind the ears. Sandee truly loved animals more than people and volunteered to foster animals in need, often traveling great distances to pick them up—something that no one knew about her.

As she stood up, her mind wandered back to the upcoming town event—the Prelude. Sandee had volunteered to manage the charity sales tent, a role that people often avoided due to its demanding nature. Between the cold weather and the long hours, it was not the most glamorous of positions. But she saw it as her chance for redemption, an opportunity to give back to the community and, perhaps, show them a different side of herself as well as a way to help animals.

If she could run the charity tent successfully, maybe, just maybe people would start to look at her differently. It wasn't about proving anything to Claire or anyone specific but rather to the town at large—and to herself. Sandee wanted to demonstrate that she could be more than the young woman who got entangled with a not-quite-single man, more than the source of a trivial dog biscuit controversy.

With a final pat to the dog, Sandee straightened her posture, her heels clicking with newfound resolve as she walked away. The road to redemption would be long, but she was ready to take that first step, and the charity tent at the Prelude seemed like the perfect place to start.

# CHAPTER SIX

B ack in the cozy, aromatic space of Sandcastles Bakery, Andie savored each bite of her caramel apple croissant, a flaky masterpiece that seemed to capture the essence of autumn in each mouthful. She looked across the table at Bunny and Sam, who were still filling in the crossword puzzle even as the three of them chatted.

"Ah, got it!" Bunny exclaimed, filling in a word on the paper. "Seven across is 'tire.'"

Sam chuckled. "Right you are!"

As he filled in the word, Bunny looked over at Andie. "Now, tell us more about this mystery."

"Well," Andie began, "I was going through these old trunks I bought at an estate sale, and I discovered something odd. There were a bunch of Christmas decorations and ornaments, but also one sad little present, still wrapped. The tag says, 'To Urchin.' No idea who Urchin is, but I feel compelled to find out more."

Bunny's eyes widened with curiosity, "A lone, unopened gift in an old trunk? That is mysterious."

"Exactly," Andie said. "I thought maybe you could help me figure out who Urchin is and maybe even give them their long-lost gift."

Sam raised his brows and looked at Bunny. "We don't have much else to do…"

"And it does sound interesting," Bunny added.

Andie's eyes sparkled at the prospect of embarking on this adventure with her friends. "So you're in?"

"Wouldn't miss it for the world," Sam affirmed, his eyes twinkling. "Where did you get the trunks? That seems like the obvious place to start."

"Iris Perkins's estate sale," Andie said, sitting back with her hands wrapped around the coffee mug.

"Ah, Iris Perkins, you say?" Bunny's eyebrows furrowed as she made a slight face. "That woman was a notorious hoarder. And she never met an estate sale she didn't like. You can't be certain those trunks originally belonged to her family."

"True," Andie conceded, "but they were hidden deep in the attic, covered in dust. It wasn't just part of the usual clutter, which makes me think they've been there for a while."

"Still," Bunny continued, "Iris could've acquired those trunks at any time and from anywhere and simply stashed them in her attic."

Sam looked thoughtful, his eyes narrowing as he mulled over the details. "Bunny has a point, but I still say we start with Perkins."

"Sounds like a plan," Bunny said. "We'll do some research, and it might really help to see what else was in the trunk."

"Oh, sure! I have it at the shop. Pop on by whenever you get a chance," Andie said.

"Hey, folks," Bert chimed in from the next table, leaning back in his chair so he could join the conversation. "Have you heard about that big storm down the Cape? Quite the whopper, they say."

Bunny frowned. "Oh no! I hope it's not going to ruin Prelude."

"Don't worry, the forecast says it's going to stay down there," Bert reassured them, glancing out the door to make sure his terrier mix Chloe was okay outside. She was sitting next to Sam's hound dog, Dooley, the two of them watching tourists stroll past. "Looks like it will be sunny here and mid-sixties, perfect for Prelude."

All eyes turned toward the window as they caught sight of volunteers and town workers stringing up twinkling lights on the lampposts and setting out paper-bag luminaries along the sidewalks.

"Excellent," Sam said, putting his hand atop Bunny's and gazing at her fondly. "This year is very special, so I'm not surprised everything will work out perfectly."

Bunny nodded. "And hopefully, we can make it extra special for the person that never got their gift all those years ago."

Just then, the door chimed, and the four women who were staying at Tides came in. They spotted Andie, their eyes lighting up with recognition.

"Oh, hi, Andie!" Susan exclaimed, walking over with her friends in tow.

"Hello there," Andie greeted them with a warm smile. "Let me introduce you to my friends Bunny and Sam." She turned to Bunny. "These ladies are guests at Tides: Betty, Susan, Margie, and Carol. They used to live in Lobster Bay."

"Hello, nice to meet you." Bunny extended her hand, her eyes sparkling with warmth.

"A pleasure," Sam echoed, nodding politely.

Bunny shifted her chair to make room. "Care to join us?"

"Oh, we'd love to, but we're actually on our way to walk the Marginal Way," Susan explained. "We just stopped in to get some Beach Bones for Cooper."

"Cooper will love that." Andie chuckled.

"Have a great walk!" Bunny replied as the four women headed to the counter to place their order.

Bunny turned her attention back to the table. She leaned in and lowered her voice. "Now, let's come up with a solid game plan for this investigation."

Andie sat back and sipped her coffee, satisfied that she'd found the right people to take on the job. She just hoped that Claire and Maxi would be able to solve their issues as easily.

BETTY PULLED her scarf a little tighter around her neck as the four friends made their way along the Marginal Way. The walkway hugged the cliffs, offering breathtaking views of the Atlantic Ocean. The ocean breeze was blustery, a reminder that fall was setting in, but somehow, it felt invigorating rather than cold.

Margie led the way, her eyes lighting up at the

sight of a bed of late-blooming flowers. "Would you look at that? Even in the fall, this place refuses to lose its charm."

Carol nodded, her hands tucked into the pockets of her cardigan. "There's something about the ocean that's eternally captivating. It's like it holds all the world's secrets."

Susan, ever the photographer of the group, stopped to capture a dramatic cluster of rocks jutting out into the ocean. "This place is a photographer's dream. Every angle is a new surprise."

Betty smiled, genuinely happy to be sharing this moment with her friends. Yet her thoughts kept drifting. When she was a teen, she and Heidi used to walk down the Marginal Way as a shortcut from their house to the beach. If there were ever a place for her to feel her sister's presence, or perhaps even receive a sign from her, this was it.

They came upon a bench that seemed to have been perfectly placed, offering a panoramic view of the main beach across the river.

"Let's take a breather," Margie suggested, brushing a stray lock of hair from her face.

They all settled onto the bench, each lost in her own thoughts as they looked out over the crashing waves, the distant beach, and the infinite horizon.

Betty felt a mix of peace and melancholy wash over her. She closed her eyes for a moment, half praying, half wishing for some form of connection. The emotion swelled in her chest, making it hard to breathe.

Suddenly, Carol nudged her softly. "Look, Betty."

A lone seagull had landed on one of the nearby rocks, its white feathers a stark contrast to the dark stone. The bird seemed to hesitate for a moment before turning its head to look directly at them.

Betty felt a shiver run down her spine. Could this be the sign she had been hoping for? She felt her heart race as she considered the possibility. Was it foolish to think that a simple seagull could be a messenger from beyond?

Margie, unaware of Betty's internal struggle, chuckled. "He's quite the poser, isn't he? It's like he's asking for his photo to be taken."

Susan, never one to miss an opportunity, lifted her camera and took a few shots of the photogenic bird.

The seagull lingered for a few more moments before taking off, its wings catching the wind as it soared away, blending into the vast sky.

Betty felt tears prick her eyes. Whether it was a sign or just a simple coincidence, it had given her a moment of unexpected but much-needed comfort. For the first time in a long while, she felt a gentle lifting of the weight she had been carrying.

Finally, Susan stood up, slinging her camera over her shoulder. "Shall we continue? There's so much more to see."

Betty nodded, rising from the bench. "Yes, let's."

As they resumed their walk, Betty took one last look at the spot where the seagull had been. She felt a newfound sense of peace as they moved forward, her friends by her side and her sister's memory tucked safely in her heart.

# CHAPTER SEVEN

"Gerard, won't you please reconsider?" Maxi pleaded, her voice tinged with desperation as she paced back and forth across the spacious gallery, passing through the patches of natural light from the floor-to-ceiling windows and skylights. The white walls around her seemed all too empty without the artwork that had been the cause of so much tension.

"My artistic sensibilities cannot allow it, Maxi," Gerard said firmly from the other end of the line. "I'll be by to collect my work as soon as that harridan Priya has removed hers."

Maxi glanced over just in time to see Priya wheeling out the last of her pieces, the door chimes ringing softly as she exited. "Fine, Gerard. I'll expect you soon, then."

With a resigned sigh, Maxi hung up the phone and flopped down into a chair. She ripped her hair out of the bun and ran her hands through it before twisting it up on top of her head again. This was a disaster. Chandler Van Beck had entrusted her with curating a special gallery event for Winter Prelude, and now she had no art to show for it.

Just then, her phone rang again. This time, the caller ID showed it was Chandler himself. Her stomach twisted in knots as she picked up the phone.

"Maxi, how are the preparations going for the gallery event? I trust all is well?" Chandler's voice was smooth but carried a weight of expectation.

Maxi hesitated for a moment, choosing her words carefully. "Everything's coming along, Chandler. I've got something special planned for the event."

"Oh? Do tell," Chandler pressed, his curiosity piqued.

Maxi felt her heart racing; she couldn't let Chandler know about the artists pulling out. "Well, it's a bit of a surprise, actually. I don't want to give too much away, but I think it's going to be something truly unique and memorable."

"A surprise, you say? I do enjoy a good surprise," Chandler responded, sounding intrigued but cautious. "Just remember, Maxi, this event is important not only for the gallery but for the cultural aspect of the Winter Prelude. I trust you'll make it exceptional. And don't forget it needs to be filled with holiday vibes and showcase a wonderful culture that people might not be familiar with."

"You won't be disappointed, Chandler. That's a promise," Maxi assured him, even as a wave of uncertainty washed over her.

"Ahh, so you are playing it close to the vest. Don't want to reveal any more details? You know I have eyes and ears around town," Chandler added casually.

Maxi felt a jolt of panic. Would someone see Priya and Gerard moving their things and tell Chandler about the empty gallery? How could she prevent that? "Of course I know that." Maxi's gaze darted around the room as she desperately tried to think about how she could spin this. A piece of paper had blown up outside and was resting against the window. It gave her an idea. "That's why I'm going the extra mile to keep it all under wraps," Maxi quickly responded, her mind racing. "The windows will be covered to maintain the element of surprise for everyone."

"I like the sound of that. Keep up the good work, Maxi," Chandler said before finally ending the call.

Maxi placed the phone on the desk, staring at it as if it were a ticking time bomb. She had just bought herself a little time, but now she had to deliver on her promise of a "surprise." She couldn't let Chandler or the community down. Winter Prelude was too important. Maxi stood up, straightened her blouse, and took a deep breath. One way or another, she was going to pull this off.

# CHAPTER EIGHT

As Jane carefully arranged an assortment of cheese and crackers on a rustic, antique wooden platter, she couldn't help but feel a deep connection to the room she was in. Tides was a place full of history. Each piece of furniture, every framed photograph, had belonged to her ancestors, and the place exuded a sense of belonging.

The room's palette was in soft shades of blue and beige, reminiscent of the ocean and sand just outside the window. The air smelled of a comforting blend of salty sea air and the earthy aroma of vintage wood furniture. One could also catch the delicate fragrance of the cheese and crackers, beckoning anyone who entered to partake.

A classical music station played softly in the background, filling the room with tranquil melodies that blended well with the rhythmic sound of waves crashing against the shore. The occasional cry of a seagull punctuated the soundscape, seamlessly intertwining nature and nurture.

The silk oriental rug underfoot still felt luxurious even though it was two hundred years old, adding a tactile richness to the room that was comforting and inviting. The armchairs and sofa had the worn-in softness that only came with years of love and use.

But it was the view that took center stage—the sky was an artist's palette of pinks and blues, melding seamlessly into the horizon. Though the sun was setting to the west, its retreating light lent a magical glow to the eastward ocean view. The hues of the sky were reflected on the surface of the ocean, making the waves look like they were dancing in a kaleidoscope of color.

Jane heard a flurry of voices in the foyer and poked her head out into the hallway to see Susan, Betty, Carol, and Margie, their arms laden with shopping bags.

"I've set up the wine and cheese for you in here!" Jane called to them.

Their eyes widened appreciatively at the view and the setting Jane had prepared.

"Jane, this is gorgeous! You must join us," Susan insisted, her eyes twinkling.

Betty chimed in, "Yes, absolutely. We could use a new person to talk to."

"And settle our bet as to who got the best gift." Margie laid her bags down and sat in an overstuffed blue chair. Even though the room was full of antiques, Jane had put in some modern furniture for comfort.

Cooper raced in and proceeded to greet each of the women, much to their delight. At least they loved having a dog at the inn. Jane had been a bit leery of having a dog there, but so far, all of the guests had loved him. If she ever did have a guest who was put off by a resident dog, she could always send him to stay with her boyfriend, Mike. Cooper was half his, after all.

Jane took a sip of her wine, savoring the robust flavor before setting her glass on the antique coffee table. "So, how was your walk along the Marginal Way? It's a bit chilly this time of year."

Carol giggled, "Oh, it was brisk, all right. But a little cold air never stopped us from enjoying the view."

Margie added, "The ocean looked so alive today. The waves were really putting on a show."

Cooper plopped himself next to Jane, his tail

wagging in slow, contented sweeps. He looked up expectantly as Betty picked up a cracker. She popped it into her mouth then looked down at the dog. "We got something for you, Cooper."

Susan reached into her bag and brought out a package of Beach Bones. She looked to Jane for confirmation before breaking one in half and holding it out to Cooper. Cooper sniffed it then took it gently and inhaled it in one gulp.

"You know, something unusual happened while we were sitting on one of the benches. A seagull landed on a rock right in front of us and just... stared at us for the longest time," Betty said.

Susan grinned, "Maybe it wanted some of the coffee we had brought along!"

Betty shook her head, her face turning somewhat introspective. "No, it felt different—special even. I couldn't help but think it might be a sign from my sister."

The smile that stretched across Betty's face was serene, as though she'd come to some unspoken agreement with the universe about her sister's passing.

The room went quiet for a moment, allowing everyone to take in the weight of Betty's words. Even Cooper seemed to sense the change in mood, resting his head gently on Jane's lap.

Carol was the first to jump in, eagerly unzipping her shopping bag. "All right, ladies, get ready to see the ultimate gift for my grandson, Jack. Ta-da!" She pulled out a quirky, colorful beach towel featuring a lighthouse scene complete with little cartoon seagulls and starfish and matching swim trunks.

"Imagine how cool he'll look at his swimming lessons with this. It's like giving him a piece of the ocean!"

Betty was next. "That's adorable, Carol, but wait until you see what I found for Emily." She carefully unwrapped a hand-carved wooden model of a lighthouse, her charm bracelet jangling. "She loves lighthouses. Just look at the craftsmanship!"

Susan chuckled as she reached into her bag. "You guys are so sentimental. I went for fun! Look at this for Lily!" She presented a quirky, oversized sun hat, complete with fake flowers and a band that read "Beach Please!"

"Her Instagram photos are going to be epic!"

Margie took the final turn. "Prepare yourselves, because I found a treasure for Ben." With a flourish, she unveiled a pirate-themed puzzle. "It's a 3D puzzle of a pirate ship, and the pieces are made from recycled materials! Ben's into that eco-friendly stuff, so this is perfect!"

Each lady reveled in the playful banter and gentle ribbing that followed, arguing lightheartedly about whose gift would make the biggest splash. Even Cooper seemed to join in, wagging his tail happily as if he, too, had an opinion on the best gift.

"So whose is best?" Carol turned to Jane.

"Ummm... well..."

"Yoo-hoo! I'm here!" a voice called from the foyer, saving Jane from having to answer.

"In here!" Jane called.

Sally stepped into the room, her tool belt slung casually around her waist and her long silver braid pulled over one shoulder. The moment she appeared, Carol, Betty, Margie, and Susan practically leapt from their seats. "Sally!"

With a hearty laugh, Sally opened her arms wide, enveloped in hugs from the women. Their chatter all blended together as Sally made the rounds. Betty broke into laughter, her eyes twinkling. "Oh my gosh, Sally! No one has called me that in ages!"

Jane had watched the heartwarming exchange, a glass of wine in one hand and Cooper by her side. Apparently, the women all knew Sally, though Jane shouldn't have been surprised. They were the same age, and Sally had grown up in Lobster Bay too.

The room was filled with a tangible sense of

community, one that extended through generations and connections, and it added a layer of warmth.

Sally finally looked at Jane, "All right, where's the window trim that needs attention?"

Jane smiled, pointing to the foyer. "It's in the foyer. I'll show you."

"I can find it." Sally rolled up her sleeves. "I'll have it fixed in a jiffy. Though I must admit, it's hard to focus on work with such good company and a view like this."

"Well, hurry up, then, and when you're done, you can join us!" Jane said.

"Oh, we have one more thing. Look at this, ladies!" Margie said.

She carefully unwrapped a small porcelain figure, a charming Victorian house situated on the beach. It bore a striking resemblance to Tides, the very inn they were in. "We got this for Addie. We always loved how welcoming she was whenever we stayed here. Thought it might brighten her day in the assisted-living facility."

Jane was touched, her eyes misty. "Oh, Margie, this is beautiful. Mom will love it. Really, she will. Cooper and I are going to visit her tomorrow morning, and this will be such a lovely surprise for her."

As she spoke, Cooper wagged his tail in agreement,

as if he, too, knew the sentimental value of the porcelain house.

"Well, then, it's settled. This little house will have
a new home, and it's the perfect way to keep Tides
always near to Addie," Carol chimed in, her glass
raised in a toast.

# CHAPTER NINE

E arly the next morning, Claire was behind the counter at Sandcastles Bakery, ringing up a string of blueberry muffins, almond croissants, and steaming cups of coffee. The cozy bakery was bustling, tables full of customers sipping lattes and savoring pastries.

Maxi burst through the door, her eyes darting around before landing on Claire. "Morning, Claire! Can I get two lemon poppyseed muffins, three raspberry scones, and a large coffee to go, please?"

Claire began to assemble the order, curiosity piqued. "You seem in a hurry. Big plans?"

"Plans? You could say that," Maxi huffed. "I'm in the middle of covering the windows at the art gallery. I'm trying to keep the new display a surprise. Plus, I've got a couple of leads on artists whose work I might be able to feature. And I only have three days to pull it all together!"

"A surprise display? That sounds exciting!" Claire handed Maxi the bag and the large coffee. "Who is helping you out?"

Maxi sighed. "No one. That's why I need all these pastries. Gotta keep up my strength."

Claire raised a brow. "If you have a few minutes, Jane should be here soon. I've got a bag of chocolate chip muffins for Addie." Claire pointed to a white bakery bag sitting on the counter.

Maxi glanced at her watch and then back at Claire. "I'd love to, but time is of the essence. I'll catch up with her tonight at girls' night. See you then!"

"All right, then. Good luck, Maxi! You've got this." Claire offered a supportive smile as Maxi rushed out, her arms full but her spirits high.

Claire watched Maxi bustle out of the bakery and almost collide with Sam, who was outside, tying Dooley to one of the dog-friendly stations Claire had set up. Dooley, a lovable hound dog with droopy ears and soulful eyes, wagged his tail as Sam patted his head. His nose quivered, catching the scent of freshly baked goods wafting from the bakery.

During the summer months, Claire allowed

patrons to bring their dogs to the outdoor eating area, and it had been an instant hit. In fact, the idea for the Beach Bones dog treat line originated from seeing how much the canines enjoyed hanging out. Now, even during the cooler months, dog stations with water bowls were placed in front of the café so people could still bring their furry friends along.

Sam walked in, the door chiming as he entered. "Morning, Claire. Could I get two bran muffins and some Beach Bones for Dooley? He seems to like the red ones."

Claire's eyebrows furrowed. Red ones? She didn't make red Beach Bones. For a moment, she wondered if Sam was confused. He was getting up in years... or had he somehow gotten hold of Sandee's Beach Bones? Were they better than hers? She pushed the thought aside.

"Red ones? That's strange. I haven't made red Beach Bones. But here are our original-recipe bones. Dooley seems to like them too, right?"

Sam chuckled. "Oh, he loves them! I must be mistaken about the color. Old age, you know?"

Claire prepared the bran muffins and Beach Bones for Sam, placing them carefully into a bag. "You're not going to sit with a crossword?" Sam and Bunny came almost every morning now and did crosswords at their favorite table.

"Actually, I'm about to pick up Bunny." Sam glanced toward the curb, where his red convertible was parked. Even in the chillier weather, he and Bunny adored the feeling of open-air driving. "We're heading over to Andie's antique shop to have a look at that old trunk she's curious about."

"Sounds good." Claire loved that Sam and Bunny kept active even though they were in their late seventies. And it was fantastic to see that spark back in Sam's eye. Claire hadn't been sure she'd ever see that again after Sam's wife passed, but then he'd met Bunny, and the rest was history.

"Thanks!" Sam held up the bag and left just as a woman approached the counter.

Claire recognized her immediately—it was Marie from the local animal rescue organization.

"Hi, Claire, how are you today?" Marie greeted her warmly.

"Doing well, Marie. What can I get for you?"

"Well, first, I wanted to give you this." Marie handed Claire a letter with the rescue organization's logo on it. "It's a thank-you letter for being such a friend to animals. The way you've made Sandcastles a pet-friendly place has really made a difference, not just to pet owners but to the animals themselves. And the Beach Bones? They're a hit at the rescue center!"

Claire's heart swelled with pride as she opened the letter and quickly skimmed it. Official recognition for her efforts made her feel even more grounded in her determination to keep the Beach Bones name.

"Oh, and one more thing," Marie continued. "I know you're going to be manning the charity tent at the Winter Prelude event, and we're so grateful for that. But would you consider doing a little more? We've got an influx of animals due to natural disasters in other parts of the country. Any chance you'd be open to fostering?"

Claire paused. She hadn't considered fostering animals before, but the idea intrigued her. "That's quite a responsibility," she said thoughtfully.

"It is, but I think you'd be amazing at it," Marie replied. "Plus you'd have a captive test audience for new Beach Bones recipes!"

Claire chuckled at that. "You make a compelling case, Marie. I'll definitely think about it."

"Great, that's all I ask. Thanks again for everything you do, Claire. Oh, I'll have a pistachio scone and a small coffee."

Claire got the scone and coffee and rang Marie up then put the letter somewhere safe. She'd have it framed. The morning rush had died down, and some of the tables were empty, so she grabbed a rag and started wiping them down.

Her phone rang. It was her daughter, Tammi.

"Hey, Tammi. How's your day going?" Tammi was doing an internship far away, and Claire missed seeing her every day, but she was proud of the woman Tammi had become.

"Busy but good. How about you?"

"Actually, amazing," Claire gushed, unable to hold back her excitement. "Marie from the animal rescue just came by and gave me this thank-you letter for being a friend to animals and the community. It feels so good to be recognized."

"That's wonderful, Mom! You deserve it," Tammi replied.

"Thanks. It makes me all the more determined to keep the Beach Bones name," Claire asserted, her voice tinged with resolve.

Tammi paused, choosing her words carefully. "Mom, you and Sandee have more in common than you think."

Claire snorted. "I highly doubt that."

"Don't be so quick to judge. Sandee's a friend to animals too. She's not the villain you think she is."

"That's hardly something substantial to have in

common," Claire retorted. "Unless you consider being married to your father something in common."

Another pause on Tammi's end had Claire worrying that she'd said the wrong thing. She'd always been careful not to be one of those divorced parents that bad-mouthed the other or their new partner.

"Actually, Dad and Sandee are getting divorced."

"Oh." Claire didn't know what to say. "Well, that's... interesting."

"Yeah, well, maybe the two of you could find some common ground, you know? Life's too short for grudges," Tammi suggested.

Claire sighed. "I'll think about it, Tammi. I really will."

Funny, Claire had always thought Sandee and Peter deserved each other. Maybe Tammi was on to something... or maybe Peter had found an even younger woman and tossed Sandee aside. Either way, it wasn't really her problem.

"Penny for your thoughts."

Claire looked up to see Jane standing at the counter.

"Oh, it's nothing." Claire quickly brushed it off, though her mind was still racing with the new revelation about Sandee and Peter. A strange mix of emotions—annoyance, curiosity, and, surprisingly, sympathy—filled her. Could Sandee also be a victim of Peter's insincerity? Claire knew all too well how that felt.

"I've got your chocolate chip muffins for Addie right here," Claire said, handing over the white paper bag.

"Ah, she's going to love these! Thank you, Claire."

"Of course. Anything for Addie," Claire replied, sharing a warm smile with Jane.

"Gotta run!" Jane turned toward the door. "See you at Barnacle Billy's tonight?"

"Absolutely! Six o'clock, and don't be late. We have a lot to catch up on."

# CHAPTER TEN

Jane stepped into her mother Addie's room, which was warm and comforting. It was filled with the familiar furniture that had once adorned their family home, each piece a treasured relic of their shared past. The bed was covered with a patchwork quilt that Jane had seen since her childhood, each square a testament to the years gone by. Outside the window, a bird feeder hung from a branch, attracting an array of colorful birds that Addie loved to watch.

Cooper ran in ahead of Jane, and Addie's face lit up. "Cooper! I always love seeing you!" Addie leaned down to pet the dog, who wiggled with delight.

Jane handed her mother the bag of chocolate chip muffins from Sandcastles Café. Addie's eyes lit up as she caught the aroma wafting from the bag.

"Oh, these smell divine! Did Claire make these?" Addie asked as she took a muffin and bit into it, savoring the taste.

"Yes, Mom, she did," Jane replied, pleased that her mother remembered her friend.

"Has she graduated from cooking school yet?" Addie inquired, her eyes shining with curiosity.

Jane felt a bittersweet emotion wash over her. "No, Mom. Claire runs her own café now, remember? She's been out of school for quite some time."

Addie looked slightly confused, as if trying to fit together pieces of a puzzle. "Ah, yes, I must've forgotten. Time flies, doesn't it?"

Jane nodded, her heart aching a little but also filled with love. "Yes, it does. Speaking of which, do you remember four women that used to come to the inn every fall? Susan, Margie, Betty, and Carol?"

Addie nodded even though the confused look in her eye told Jane she didn't really remember them.

"They wanted me to give you this." Jane pulled the little figurine out of her bag.

Addie's eyes lit up. "It looks like Tides!" Addie took the figurine from Jane and admired it for a few minutes before giving it a prominent place on her bookshelf. "I'll keep it right here where I can see it all the time. Will you thank them for me?"

"I will."

Addie took another bite of her muffin and then glanced around her room. "They've started decorating for the Winter Prelude. Would you like to take a walk and see the decorations in the common rooms?"

"I'd love to. Mike is supposed to meet me here to take Cooper back to his place. Why don't we wait for him?"

"Sure. I can finish my muffin."

Hearing a soft knock on the door, they turned to see Mike standing there. Jane and Mike had been dating for a few months now, and the sight of him still made her heart flip. Cooper rushed over to Mike, and the man bent down to lavish the dog with attention.

"Hey, boy! I missed you." Mike rubbed Cooper's fur then stood and gave Jane a soft kiss on the cheek. "And you too."

"And me?" Addie asked innocently.

Mike laughed. "Especially you." He walked over and kissed Addie on top of the head.

"I was just telling Jane that they've started putting up the decorations for the Winter Prelude," Addie chimed in. "Maybe we can all go take a look?"

Jane, Mike, and Addie wandered through the common areas of Tall Pines Assisted Living. The soft glow of twinkling white lights washed over them, lending a magical touch to the surroundings. From the art room to the library, each space seemed transformed into a cozy winter wonderland.

When they reached the puzzle room, they heard a voice tinged with concern say, "Now, Mom, this is too much. You should take it easy."

An unmistakable Norwegian accent shot back, "Hush up. I'm perfectly fine and full of energy!"

Rounding the corner, they came upon Olga Svenson and another woman standing among a flurry of festive decorations. Olga was arranging an intricate ornament on a shelf.

"Ah, Jane! So good to see you!" Olga beamed. "I hope you are enjoying the decorations I gave Liz for the Inn. Meet my daughter, Kristina."

"Nice to meet you, Kristina," Jane said warmly then turned to Olga. "Thank you so much for sending of the decorations. They look fantastic, and my guests love them."

"You're very welcome, dear. I have more. It gets lonely just sitting around all day, so I've been getting into the holiday spirit early." Olga's sapphire eyes twinkled.

Kristina sighed. "Mom, really, you're doing too much for your age. The decorating, the baking, managing the house—it's a lot. Maybe it's time to consider a nice room here at Tall Pines."

Olga's eyes narrowed, her gaze full of defiance. "Not a chance, young lady. I have more energy than people half my age and love to keep busy!"

Addie, who had been quietly observing the exchange, finally spoke. "Oh, let Olga be. As long as she's able, she should do what makes her happy. You never know when you might not be able to do things or even take care of your own home anymore."

Her words hung in the air, carrying a weight that seemed to hit home for everyone in the room. Kristina looked at her mother, perhaps seeing her in a new light, while Olga nodded appreciatively at Addie's insight.

# CHAPTER ELEVEN

In the warm, cozy ambiance of Andie's antique store, Sam and Bunny were seated in front of the old trunk in which Andie had found the unopened gift. Antique furniture and vintage collectibles surrounded them, each with a story of its own. Dooley sat obediently nearby, his keen eyes watching the proceedings.

Sam carefully lifted the lid of the trunk, revealing a mishmash of items—a true time capsule. Bunny, her eyes shining with curiosity, was the first to reach inside. She pulled out an old Raggedy Ann doll and some doilies.

"I don't think Iris even went through this. You know, sometimes, she would come back on a Saturday afternoon with her car full and just fill up her spare room. I wonder how many of her treasures she never even looked at again," Bunny mused.

"No wonder her kids just wanted to have a big sale to clean it all out." Sam reached into the trunk and carefully pulled out an old 45 record. "I hear the place was packed full."

"It was." Andie remembered having to pick her way through the piles of stuff at the sale.

Bunny pulled out a set of old linens, beautifully embroidered but showing signs of age. "Oh! Look at these!" Bunny exclaimed, holding the linens up to the light. "They're exquisite, but they have a D embroidered on them. That can't be from the Perkins family."

"What was Iris's maiden name?" Sam asked.

"Brown," Bunny replied without even looking up from the trunk. "But that's a good thought. It could be one of the related families. That should be easy to find out in the town records at the library."

Sam agreed. "And these old newspapers might have some clues." He pulled out a stack of yellowed papers dated from fifty-five years ago. "We can look through town records or old newspapers to find a family with a D in their name."

"And these bulletins from St. Mary's church. Whoever had this trunk must have belonged to the congregation," Bunny added.

As Bunny and Sam continued to sift through the trunk, their hands landed on a variety of items that instantly transported them back to their own childhoods. Sam pulled out a View-Master, complete with scenic reels.

"I had one of these!" he exclaimed, peering through it for a moment. "Hey, these are antiques?"

Bunny laughed as she examined an old rotary-dial phone, lifting it as if she was going to make a call. "I guess that makes you an antique, too, Sam."

Dooley seemed to catch the jest, letting out an excited bark as if he understood the humor.

The room filled with laughter, which echoed warmly through the store.

"Ah, well, if I'm an antique, I'm a well-preserved one," Sam joked, giving Bunny a playful nudge.

As Bunny carefully folded the old linens back into the trunk, Sam neatly stacked the yellowed newspapers on top.

"So, we'll start by looking through the Perkins family tree to see if there is a branch whose last name begins with D," Sam said, outlining their plan. "And if that doesn't pan out, we'll start in on the town files to look for families whose last name begins with a D."

"Right," Bunny confirmed. "Then we should probably speak with some of the older residents. They might remember something useful. Olga, for instance, seems to have the memory of an elephant."

"And after that, if we come up with any potential families, we could dig a little deeper. Maybe look into estate sales or yard sales around that time," Sam added, latching the trunk closed.

"Those are great ideas. What can I help with?" Andie asked.

Bunny and Sam exchanged a glance.

"You just leave it to us, dear. We have a process, and you're busy here at the shop anyway." Bunny glanced at Sam. "What do you say we hit the library?"

Sam stood and stretched. "Great idea. I always say there's no time like the present to get started on an investigation."

# CHAPTER TWELVE

M axi carefully adjusted the last piece of paper covering the gallery windows. Peeking through a tiny gap, she caught sight of the Winter Prelude festivities happening outside. Stores were setting up tables brimming with holiday merchandise, and twinkling lights adorned windows and lampposts. The cheerful ambiance made her stomach churn with nervous anticipation; she still hadn't found the perfect artist for her gallery showing.

Her gaze shifted to the bright sign she had put up outside: "Grand Reveal Saturday!" Passersby stopped to read it, their curiosity evident as they tried to look through the covered windows. Maxi felt a mix of excitement and sheer panic. Time was running out, and she still had no art to reveal. She did, however, have some prospects, and one of them, Una Thomas, was supposed to be here any minute. Maxi had never heard of the woman, but she'd answered an ad Maxi had put up at the artists' café, and Maxi was desperate enough to talk to anyone.

Just then, the door swung open, and a woman walked in, looking around in confusion. She spotted Maxi and smiled.

"Hi, I'm Una," she said. She pulled a wheeled suitcase behind her. "Ready to have your mind blown?"

"Absolutely," Maxi said, eager but also apprehensive. "What do you have for us?"

Una unzipped her suitcase and pulled out what looked like a Christmas wreath, but upon closer inspection, Maxi noticed it was made entirely of mini voodoo dolls adorned with holiday hats and scarves. Each was carefully pinned with tiny mistletoe leaves and holly berries.

"It's a cross-cultural celebration," Una explained, beaming. "Louisiana voodoo meets holiday cheer!"

Maxi's eyes widened. While she couldn't deny the cultural infusion and festive element, the artwork was also downright eerie.

"Imagine an entire gallery filled with these!" Una exclaimed as she pulled out a giant doll with a knife through its right eye.

Maxi hesitated, trying to find the right words. "It's... very unique, and certainly embraces a cross-cultural theme," she said cautiously, "but I'm not sure it's got the festive vibe we're looking for."

Una looked slightly deflated but nodded in understanding. "Oh, well...." She glanced around the empty gallery.

"Thanks for coming by." Maxi walked her to the door. "I'll be in touch."

After Una left, Maxi sighed and flopped into the chair behind the desk. Hopefully, she wouldn't have to resort to a gallery full of voodoo dolls wearing garland and tinsel.

Her phone buzzed on the counter. It was Muriel, a well-connected artist friend of hers.

"Maxi! I just got your message," Muriel chirped. "I think I've found someone for the gallery showing."

"Oh, that would be fantastic."

"I don't know her personally, but her name is Elana Brussels. I heard that she has a very interesting blend of local Maine heritage and holiday cheer. Can she drop by tomorrow afternoon?"

"I have an art lesson with Bunny at four, but any time before that is good." Maxi loved the painting lessons she took with Bunny and didn't want to miss one if she could help it.

"Okay. How about two? I'll tell Todd to relay the message to her," Muriel said.

"Sounds perfect." Maxi's spirits lifted considerably. Muriel had a variety of interesting contacts, so Elana was bound to work out. She couldn't be as bad as the last person.

"Great. Let's get together soon." They said their goodbyes and hung up.

Maxi had a half hour before she had to head to Barnacle Billy's to meet the others, and that was just enough time to give her husband a quick FaceTime call.

As she held her phone in front of her, Maxi felt a rush of affection when she saw James's familiar face on the screen. Picasso and Rembrandt, their black-and-white cats, darted about in the background, their youthful energy evident even through the small screen.

"So, how's your day been?" James asked after they'd laughed at the cats' antics. "Any luck finding the perfect artist for the gallery showing?"

Maxi sighed, rolling her eyes for comedic effect. "You wouldn't believe the candidates I've had to interview. One artist came in with Christmas-themed voodoo dolls."

James chuckled. "Well, the search for art is much

like the creation of art itself—full of surprises and challenges."

"Very poetic, James." Maxi smiled. "And how's your day?"

"Busy with meetings, but it's winding down. Picasso and Rembrandt have been keeping me entertained," he said, pausing to reach down and pick up Picasso, who had decided that moment to pounce on James's foot. "So, girls' night out tonight, huh?"

"Yes, we're meeting up at Barnacle Billy's. You know how much I love our girls' nights," Maxi said, her eyes lighting up at the thought of an evening spent with her close friends.

"I do, and I'm glad you have them. Everyone needs a break and some quality time with friends," James replied warmly. "But I'll still miss you."

"I'll miss you too," Maxi said, her voice softening. "But I won't be too late, promise."

"Don't worry, Picasso and Rembrandt will keep me company."

"Thanks." Maxi smiled, touched by his understanding and support.

"See you when you get home. Love you."

"Love you too," Maxi said, ending the call with a satisfied sigh before grabbing her big striped tote bag and heading off to Barnacle Billy's.

# CHAPTER THIRTEEN

Jane pushed open the door to Barnacle Billy's, her stomach grumbling at the aroma of freshly grilled seafood.

The restaurant was alive with a symphony of sounds. From the low murmur of conversations among diners, punctuated by the occasional hearty laugh, to the soft clinking of glasses and utensils against fine china, each noise contributed to the inviting atmosphere.

She saw Claire, Maxi, and Andie seated at a table and started across the blue carpet toward them.

"Hey, ladies!" she greeted as she pulled out a chair and sat down.

"Jane, you made it! We were just about to order some wine," Claire said, her eyes lighting up. She gestured to the menus laid out on the crisp white linen tablecloth. In the middle of the table, a single candle flickered, casting a warm glow that softened their faces.

The row of windows behind them looked out onto Perkins Cove, where fishing boats and dinghies bobbed peacefully in the water. The footbridge could be seen at the mouth of the cove, and though they often dined on the patio to enjoy the view, the cooler weather had them inside tonight.

"What's everyone feeling—red, white, or sparkling?" Andie inquired, flipping through the wine list.

"I'm in the mood for a nice Chardonnay," Maxi chimed in.

"Sounds perfect. White it is," Claire confirmed, nodding at Jane for agreement. Jane offered a warm smile and nodded.

The waitress appeared and introduced herself as Sarah, and they ordered their wine.

Andie turned to Jane. "Did you visit Mom? How was she?"

"Great as usual," Jane said. "They're decorating Tall Pines for Prelude, too, and Mom seemed to like that."

"That's great. I'm glad we made the right decision putting her there," Andie said.

"We did, and speaking of decorating, I saw the paper up on the windows of the gallery when I walked by earlier, Maxi. Were you able to straighten things out with the artists for the event?"

Maxi shook her head, waiting for the waitress to set their basket of bread and wine down before answering, her voice lowered so no one could overhear. "No, unfortunately. I'm in the process of looking for new talent, and let me tell you, it's been quite the adventure. The themes some artists have been suggesting are —well, they're out there."

"Like how out there?" Claire asked, curious.

Maxi leaned in, as if sharing a secret. "Okay, so imagine this: one artist had these garish voodoo dolls with Christmas-themed clothes and mistletoe—"

Jane made a face, "Really?"

Yes!" Maxi took another sip of her wine. "So I struck out today, but Muriel found someone that might work out, and I'm going to talk to her tomorrow."

"Oh, that's good. I hope things work out." Claire flipped open her menu, and the others followed suit while discussing the different options. Once they'd decided and put the menus down, Sarah appeared.

"Looks like you ladies are ready to order. May I

interest you in tonight's special? We have a beautiful swordfish steak, grilled to perfection and served with a citrus-herb sauce."

"That sounds delicious," Claire commented, her eyes scanning the menu one last time.

"Do you all know what you'd like?" Sarah asked, pulling out her notepad.

"I'll take the swordfish special," Claire decided, closing her menu.

"I'll have the lobster tail, please," Jane said, already imagining the rich, buttery flavor.

"And I'll go for the seared scallops," Andie chimed in, smiling at Sarah.

"I'm in the mood for shrimp scampi," Maxi added, handing her menu to the waitress.

"Excellent choices," Sarah said, scribbling down their orders. "Would you like some bread for the table?"

"Of course," Jane answered for the group, earning approving nods from her friends.

"Very well. I'll get your orders in right away," Sarah said before heading back to the kitchen.

As she left, Maxi turned to Claire. "Enough about me. Tell us the latest in the Beach Bones saga."

Claire sighed as she buttered a piece of warm, crusty bread from the basket Sarah had deposited in the center of the table. "You won't believe it, but Sandee actually had the nerve to come into my store today. And no, we didn't resolve anything. We're both as stubborn as mules."

"That's tough," Maxi said sympathetically. "I can't even imagine having to deal with that level of tension."

Claire took a bite of the bread, contemplating her next words. "You know, sometimes, I wonder if I'm just being silly about the whole thing. But when I try to approach her rationally, she just... I don't know, makes it difficult."

"Well, you'll get another chance to sort it out," Andie chimed in with a mischievous grin.

Claire looked puzzled. "What do you mean?"

"You really don't know?" Andie's eyes twinkled with amusement. "Both of you are on the roster to man the charity tent for the animal shelter tomorrow. You'll be side by side for the entire afternoon."

Claire's eyes widened, the piece of bread frozen in midair. "You're kidding. Please tell me you're kidding."

"Nope, it's happening," Andie confirmed, taking a sip of her wine. "Who knows, maybe things will work out."

Claire snorted. "More like there'll be a brawl."

Everyone laughed.

"Maybe she really isn't that bad if she's volunteering to work the charity tent," Jane said.

"Maybe." Claire didn't look convinced. "Tammi said we did have a lot in common, and I guess Sandee and Peter are getting divorced."

"What?" Maxi looked surprised.

"Yeah, I had no idea. Tammi sounded like she even felt sorry for her," Claire said. "Maybe I should give her a chance."

"You never know, could be a new friendship." Jane dipped a piece of lobster tail in butter.

"Doubtful." Claire forked off a piece of swordfish. "What about you, Jane? How are your guests working out? I hope you don't have drama like me and Maxi."

"Thankfully, there's no drama at the inn. The guests are absolutely lovely, and guess what? They all know Sally!"

"Doesn't everyone know Sally?" Claire quipped, and they all laughed.

"How about you, Andie? What's going on at the store?" Maxi asked.

"No drama, but I do have a little bit of a mystery."

"Oh?" They all looked intrigued as Andie told them about the present she'd found in the trunk. "I have Sam and Bunny helping me try to find out who it belongs to."

"Bunny and Sam, eh?" Claire grinned. "They're so cute together."

"They're quite the pair, aren't they?" Jane chimed in, nibbling on a piece of bread. "Every time I see them together, it just warms my heart."

Andie nodded. "They really are good together. It's like they're both rediscovering their zest for life, and it's adorable to see. It's one of those late-in-life romances that gives everyone hope."

"Well, I hope you find the owner. That would be cool to get a gift that was meant to come years ago," Maxi said. "I have a lesson with Bunny tomorrow night after I interview that new artist. Maybe she'll have solved the mystery by then."

"I hope your new artist works out okay," Claire said to Maxi.

"Thanks, and I hope your special time with Sandee turns out okay too," Maxi teased.

Jane raised her glass. "I hope everything works out great for everyone. Here's to good friends, easy solutions, and great meals."

# CHAPTER FOURTEEN

As Sam and Bunny stepped out of the library, leaves from the oak trees that lined the street cascaded down like golden confetti, greeting them in the crisp evening air. The town was a warm, inviting scene: twinkle lights adorned trees, streetlamps, and even the front windows of quaint local shops. Pumpkins were placed here and there, some elaborately carved with faces or designs that reflected the spirit of the season.

Bunny looked around and sighed. "Isn't it just beautiful? Fall is my favorite time of the year, especially with the Winter Prelude approaching."

Sam smiled, inhaling deeply as if to absorb the essence of the season. "I love it too. The whole town seems to come alive."

Their eyes met, holding a moment of shared contentment. Then Bunny brought them back to the task at hand. "Well, we didn't get as many leads as I'd hoped. But we do have a hefty list of yard and estate sales from the classified sections of the old papers."

Sam chuckled. "Yes. If only we could narrow it down to a specific year, it'd make our search a whole lot easier."

Bunny's eyes lit up, and she nudged him playfully. "Oh, I'm sure we'll be able to figure it out. Remember how I brilliantly deduced the identity of Jane's mysterious guest a few weeks ago?"

Sam raised an eyebrow, looking amused. "Hmm, that's one version of the story. My recollection is a little different."

"Are you implying that you had a hand in that particular stroke of genius?" Bunny teased.

"Let's call it a team effort," Sam said, grinning. He patted Bunny's hand gently. "But you are undeniably sharp and very good at investigating. It's one of the many things I adore about you."

The flattery made Bunny blush, but she didn't mind one bit. "Well, thank you, Sam."

Sam grew more serious. "Look, I have an idea. When I was on the force, we often had to sift through lots of information quickly. I think we should put everything we know into a spreadsheet and then look for patterns. It might help us zero in on the right yard sale."

Bunny nodded enthusiastically. "Oh, I like that! Very organized, very systematic. It sounds perfect."

Just then, they ran into Earl, an old friend who was busy setting up paper luminaries along Main Street. The lanterns were carefully placed to lead up to the entrances of various businesses. Battery-operated candles sat inside each, ensuring there was no fire risk.

"Earl! What are you up to?" Bunny greeted him warmly.

"Hey there, you two! Just setting up for the luminary walk tomorrow night."

"It looks wonderful," Bunny remarked.

"Thanks! Lucky thing that big storm brewing is staying down near New York City and not coming up this way. Rain would ruin all our hard work with these luminaries."

Sam nodded. "Not to mention put a damper on the Prelude event."

Just as they were about to continue their walk, Marie from the animal rescue came rushing up to them, her face flushed and her eyes filled with urgency.

"Sam, Bunny, I'm so glad I caught you!" she panted, trying to catch her breath.

"What's the matter, Marie?" Sam asked, concern evident in his voice.

"It's the storm down in New York City. It's causing all kinds of problems, and many animals have been displaced. Shelters there are overwhelmed. We're coordinating efforts to provide them with some relief. I might need fosters, but I have no idea how to get the animals in need up here."

Bunny's eyes widened at the gravity of the situation, but Marie immediately clarified, "Oh, no, I don't want you guys to drive down. It's too dangerous to go right into the storm. I just meant in general, we're looking for volunteers."

Sam looked conflicted. "I'm not sure about fostering another animal. I've already got Dooley, you know."

Bunny gave his hand a reassuring squeeze. "Well, I could foster. You know I've been thinking about getting a pet anyway. This could be the perfect way to make a meaningful contribution."

Marie's eyes lit up. "Oh, Bunny, that would be such a big help. Fostering not only provides these animals with a temporary home but also makes room for other displaced animals in the shelter."

Sam nodded, appreciative of Bunny's willingness. "That sounds like a great idea. If you're fostering, I can at least help out with supplies and maybe even offer some logistical support. Dooley might not appreciate a new roommate, but I bet he'd be okay with sharing his toys."

Marie let out a sigh of relief. "You two are life-savers. I'll get everything set up and let you know if I need you to foster. I hope there won't be too many animals, in which case you guys are off the hook."

Marie rushed off, and Sam and Bunny looked at each other. "Looks like we're going to be very busy the next few days."

# CHAPTER FIFTEEN

Sandee gripped the steering wheel tightly as she navigated the treacherous roads, rain pelting against the windshield like an unyielding drumbeat. Her wipers worked in overdrive, swiping away water just fast enough for her to catch fleeting glimpses of the road ahead.

Her phone buzzed in the cup holder beside her. It was Marie, and she clicked on the speakerphone option, careful to keep her eyes on the road.

"Sandee, are you okay? This storm is crazy!"

"I'm fine, Marie," Sandee assured her, her voice tinged with a steely determination. "Someone had to go down to rescue those dogs, so it might as well be me. I'll take as many as can fit in the car."

"Please be careful," Marie urged. "The roads are treacherous."

"I will," Sandee assured her. "Look, with this weather, I think it might be best if I stay the night here. I'll try to make it back in time to man the charity tent tomorrow."

"All right," Marie agreed, her voice tinged with relief. "Just make sure you're safe, okay? Those dogs need you, but we do too."

"I will, don't worry." She hung up, her heart swelling at Marie's concern. At least someone needed her.

Her car hit a puddle, causing her to hydroplane. Her heart leapt into her throat as she lost control, the car spinning briefly before landing in a ditch beside the road. The jolt from the impact cut her conversation short, her phone falling from the cup holder and onto the car floor.

For a moment, Sandee sat there, stunned. The rain continued its relentless drumming against the roof, a stark contrast to the silence that enveloped her in the aftermath of the crash. She took a deep breath, feeling her heartbeat gradually return to normal.

Still gripping the steering wheel, Sandee stared at the rain-soaked road ahead, her thoughts swirling like the storm outside. She took a deep, shaky breath, gathering her composure.

"All right, Sandee, it's just a bump in the road. You've navigated through worse," she muttered to herself, her voice barely audible over the rain's relentless patter.

She glanced at her reflection in the rearview mirror. The woman staring back hadn't been brave enough to face a challenge like this in the past. The old Sandee would have given up at the slightest hint of trouble. She'd floated through life sheltered and pampered. But she was a different person now. The mess with Peter, the tension with Claire over Beach Bones, and now this ditch on a stormy night; they were all hurdles, but none was insurmountable.

Sandee's eyes narrowed as she surveyed the ditch her car was stuck in. Maybe, just maybe, she could get herself out of this jam without waiting for the tow truck. She gripped the steering wheel, took a deep breath, and gently pressed on the gas. The car's wheels spun in the slick mud, throwing muck and water into the air.

For a moment, it felt hopeless—the wheels just couldn't gain traction. But the new Sandee wasn't about to give up that easily. She eased off the gas, rocked back a little, and then pressed down again, giving it another go.

The car lurched, rocked back, and—yes!—slowly started to crawl its way up and out of the ditch. Sandee felt a surge of triumph as her tires hit the pavement. With one last spin, she straightened the car out onto the roadway.

"Ha! Take that!" she exclaimed, her face lighting up with a grin of pure satisfaction.

She took a second to catch her breath, her heart still racing from the adrenaline. Then, with renewed determination, she carefully navigated back onto the road, determined more than ever to help save those dogs.

# CHAPTER SIXTEEN

T he next morning, the dining room at the Inn at Tides was bustling with life. Betty, Susan, Carol, and Margie were seated at a round table draped in white linen, bathed in the morning sunlight that streamed through the large bay windows. Brenda, the inn's talented chef, walked in with a steaming plate of fluffy pancakes and set it down in front of them with a proud smile.

"Here you go, ladies, fresh off the griddle!"

Jane followed her, coffee pot in hand. "Would anyone like some more coffee?"

The four women erupted in compliments for Brenda. "These pancakes look amazing!" Susan said, the smell of maple syrup filling the air.

"Oh, Brenda, you've outdone yourself," Margie added, eagerly taking a pancake off the stack.

Brenda beamed. "Well, I'm glad you ladies are pleased. Anything to make your stay special."

After topping off everyone's coffee cups, Jane joined the conversation. "So, what's on the agenda for today? The town is buzzing with excitement for the first day of Winter Prelude."

"First things first: we're going to Spoiled Rotten," Carol declared. "I heard they're having a sale on their Lobster Bay candles. We absolutely have to get one each."

"That's definitely first," Betty agreed, sipping her coffee. "The fragrance is just so reminiscent of here. It's like taking a piece of Lobster Bay back home."

"And you're going to love the little gift bags they're giving away," Jane added, a gleam in her eyes. "Filled with local goodies."

"Of course we want to hit all the shops. I know there are such good deals during Prelude." Betty poured maple syrup on her pancake.

"Have you all noticed the lights and luminaries along Main Street?" Margie asked, taking a sip of her coffee. "The town looks so magical."

"Yes, and the pumpkins!" Carol added. "Some

people are really talented with their carving. I saw a few that were genuine works of art."

"I love how everyone gets into the spirit," Susan said. "And it's the perfect weather for our cozy fall sweaters and boots. I'm glad I brought mine, though I may have overpacked."

"You definitely overpacked," Carol joked, and everyone laughed.

Jane smiled, enjoying how everyone seemed to appreciate the little details that made Lobster Bay special. "The decorations really bring the community together. It's like the entire town is giving you a warm hug."

They all agreed, caught up in the heartwarming ambiance of the season.

"Oh, by the way, where's Cooper? He's usually here, begging for a morsel or two," Carol inquired, looking around for the friendly pooch.

"He's with Mike today," Jane said.

"Oh, how lovely. I hope he'll be back before we leave," Susan said.

As they finished their coffee and pushed their empty plates away, Susan glanced out of the window, where the sky was brightening into a beautiful, clear day. "You know, ladies, since we'll already be out and about, maybe we should take a ride to the Rachel Carson Preserve at dusk to see the deer. It'll be the perfect ending to our day."

"Oh, I love the preserve!" Carol's eyes twinkled with nostalgia. "My sisters and I used to love going there to see the deer at dusk. There was something magical about it, especially this time of year."

"I know what you mean," Margie agreed. "We used to walk the paths there all the time on weekends with my family. My dad was a big fan of all the different trees, and he'd teach us the names. Of course, I've forgotten most of them now, but those moments were special."

Susan chimed in, "And the leaves! Even though many have already fallen, the remaining ones create such a vibrant tapestry of colors. It's like the trees are putting on a final show before winter sets in."

Carol nodded, smiling warmly. "Yes, the shades of amber and crimson against the backdrop of evergreens — it's like a painting, only better because it's real. And the deer seem to love the tranquility too."

Betty's eyes softened at the memory. "And those moments when a deer would just suddenly appear in the clearing, almost like a spirit animal—it's as if the forest shared one of its best-kept secrets with you."

The table went quiet for a moment, each lost in

her own thoughts and memories of days gone by and simple pleasures.

"And then after that, how about dinner at Oarweeds?" Carol asked.

Betty sat back and patted her stomach. "I can't even think about food right now."

Margie patted her hand. "Well, if I know you, you'll be more than ready to eat by dinnertime."

Betty laughed. "True."

Susan pushed back her chair. "Let's go upstairs and get ready. We have a big day ahead of us."

After the ladies went upstairs, Jane cleared the dishes from the dining room, and she and Brenda wiped down the kitchen counters, the residual aroma of fresh pancakes and coffee filling the air. As she placed the last of the dishes in the dishwasher, her thoughts returned to the previous night's dinner with Maxi, Andie, and Claire.

The news that Claire and Sandee would be manning the animal shelter charity tent together had been a bombshell. Given their history and lingering tension, Claire was definitely going to need some moral support. And what better way to provide that than to show up as a united front?

Jane double-checked her apron, hanging it care-fully on the hook by the kitchen door, and stepped out into the crisp autumn air. A walk on the beach first would be nice, and then she'd venture to the charity tent. She didn't want Sandee to feel ganged up on, but if there was going to be trouble, her loyalties were with Claire.

# CHAPTER SEVENTEEN

Maxi paced the empty gallery, her soft-soled shoes squeaking on the floor. It was the first day of Winter Prelude, and the clock was ticking down to tomorrow's opening. She glanced around at the barren walls that were crying out for art. But maybe, just maybe Elana Brussels would be the answer to her prayers. Muriel had suggested her, and Muriel had a good eye for talent.

Just as she was in the middle of this thought, the front door creaked open, and in walked Elana. The woman was an interesting ensemble of colors and textures. She wore a patchwork skirt of various fabrics, paired with a knitted sweater featuring every shade of blue imaginable. A rainbow of bangles adorned her wrists, clinking softly as she moved. Her hair was a wild, untamed curling mass, punctuated with random small braids adorned with tiny seashells.

The woman looked around uncertainly, a frown creasing her face as she noticed how empty the gallery was. Her gaze stopped on Maxi, and she smiled.

"Ah, you must be Maxi." Elana beamed, offering a hand decorated with paint-splattered nails. "So pleased to meet you."

"Nice to meet you too, Elana," Maxi replied, shaking her hand cautiously. "So, what kind of artwork do you specialize in?"

"Well," Elana began, her eyes twinkling, "I create Christmas-themed artwork, but with a local Maine flair."

Maxi felt a moment of hope. That sounded perfect for the Winter Prelude event. "That sounds intriguing," she encouraged.

Elana's eyes brightened even more as she opened a large portfolio bag. "Allow me to show you," she said, pulling out several pieces wrapped in tissue paper. She carefully unwrapped the first, revealing what looked like a Santa Claus figure—except, upon closer inspection, Maxi realized that Santa was actually assembled from lobster claws.

"This one I call *Santa Claws*," Elana said, grinning.

Maxi blinked. The piece was kitschy, to say the least. The red lobster claws had been arranged in the shape of Santa's arms, legs, and head. The shell of the lobster tail made the body. And it emitted a faint aroma that Maxi couldn't ignore: it smelled like old, sour seafood.

Elana unveiled the next piece, this one featuring a Christmas tree made entirely out of the ends of the lobster tails, adorned with miniature buoys as ornaments. "And this," she declared, "is *O Lobster Tree.*"

Maxi suppressed a sigh. This was decidedly not what she had in mind for her gallery's Winter Prelude showcase.

"The art has a unique scent because it's authentic," Elana added as if reading Maxi's thoughts. "Smells like a real Lobster Bay Christmas, doesn't it?"

"Ah, yes." Maxi forced a polite smile. "Very authentic."

Elana went on to show her more in the same vein—a lobster-shell Rudolph and a miniature nativity scene made out of tiny lobster legs.

"Wow, these are certainly unique," Maxi finally managed to say, trying to maintain her composure. "I've never seen anything like them."

Elana looked pleased. "So, what do you think? Perfect for your showing, right? Muriel said you wanted something holiday themed but with a cultural flair, and what could be more cultural here in Maine than lobster?"

Maxi hesitated, searching for the right words. These pieces were undoubtedly unique, but they were not the elegant, refined artwork she had envisioned for her gallery. And she'd wanted something cultural that people could learn from, that would show how holidays were celebrated in a different time or a different place. How could she let Elana down gently?

"You know, Elana," she began cautiously, "your work is certainly one of a kind, but I'm not sure it's the right fit for this showing. Thank you for showing it to me, though."

Elana looked a bit deflated but nodded understandingly. "Well, art is subjective, isn't it?"

"Yes." Maxi sighed inwardly. "It certainly is."

As Elana packed up her lobster-claw creations, Maxi's mind raced. She was back to square one, and time was running out.

Maxi stood in the center of her art gallery, surrounded by empty walls that echoed her own sense of defeat. Her fingertips traced the edge of her cell phone, contemplating the awkward calls she might have to make. Should she ring up Priya or Gerard and plead for them to showcase their art on such short notice? The weight of potential failure pressed on her; the last thing she wanted was to let Chandler down.

Maxi sighed and moved toward the window, carefully peeling back a corner of the paper covering the glass. Outside, Winter Prelude was in full swing—children were laughing, couples in bright scarves and pom-pommed hats strolled arm in arm, and shops were bustling with holiday shoppers. The atmosphere was so jubilant, so hopeful, contrasting sharply with the emptiness of her gallery.

Then her eyes caught sight of the charity tent a little way down the street. Probably the only person doing worse than her was Claire. She was in the tent, awkwardly sharing the space with Sandee.

Perhaps she should go over and lend Claire some moral support. In Lobster Bay, community meant everything, and right now, one of her best friends was in the trenches.

Taking a last glance at her vacant gallery, Maxi grabbed her coat and scarf. "Who knows," she mused aloud to the empty room, "maybe a bit of goodwill can turn both our days around."

# CHAPTER EIGHTEEN

Bunny was so busy thinking about the mystery of the present that she practically ran Maxi over when she came out of the side street that housed the art gallery.

"Oh, Maxi, I'm so sorry!" Bunny exclaimed, steadying a bag filled with notebooks and papers. "I didn't see you coming out of the gallery."

"Oh, no worries. I wasn't watching where I was going," Maxi said.

Bunny's eyes darted toward the gallery's papered-up windows. "So, is everything in there still a top-secret project?"

Maxi let out a tired sigh. "Well, sort of... Let's just say it's a work in progress. I promise, I'll fill you in during our painting lesson later. Right now, I'm off to rescue Claire in the animal rescue charity tent."

"Oh dear. I heard about the storm. Those poor animals." Bunny frowned. "But why does Claire need rescuing?"

Maxi leaned in closer, lowering her voice as if sharing a state secret. "She's manning the animal rescue charity tent with Sandee. Do you know about the whole Beach Bones fiasco?"

"Unfortunately, yes." Bunny nodded. "I was hoping they'd work things out, you know? Dooley absolutely loves those treats."

"Same here," Maxi agreed, "but from what I hear, there's still a lot of tension between them. So I'm heading over there to provide some emotional backup."

Bunny smiled warmly at Maxi. "That's very kind of you, Maxi. I'll see you at four for our painting lesson."

"Looking forward to it," Maxi said, waving as Bunny continued down the cobblestone street.

As Bunny made her way to meet Sam, her thoughts kept drifting back to the Beach Bones debacle. Sam had mistakenly bought Sandee's Beach Bones from the market, thinking they were Claire's. Dooley had taken to them immediately. In fact, Dooley seemed to prefer the red ones from Sandee's collection over Claire's. Though she would never tell Claire that!

"Bunny! Over here!" Sam's voice broke through her reverie as she saw him standing near the entrance of the town library, holding two cups of steaming coffee.

"Hey!" she called back, waving and increasing her pace to reach him.

As she took the coffee cup from Sam, they shared a quick kiss.

"Did you find anything more?" Sam asked. They'd split up the detective work, with Bunny going to some of the local auction companies and Sam researching the items in the trunk further.

Bunny shook her head, a wisp of her hair falling into her eyes. "The auction houses didn't really have much. I asked to search back on what ones Olga attended, but that long ago, there were no computerized records. How about you?"

Sam shook his head. "Everything in the trunk is fairly common. So we know the people were not wealthy, at least I don't think so. But the items were a little mismatched, as if they were thrown in from different rooms or something."

Bunny sipped coffee, and an idea occurred to her. "You know, the problem is that there is too broad a time span. Maybe we should focus on the wrapping paper on the gift. If we can identify the pattern or the style of wrapping, we might be able to find out which years that paper was popular. That'll help us narrow down the yard sales we have to look at."

Sam's face lit up, "That's brilliant, Bunny!"

"I have a picture of the present on my phone. Let's get into the library and start poking around on their internet. Who knows? Maybe we'll get lucky."

Sam gave her a hug and smiled down at her. "I already got lucky when I met you."

Bunny smiled back, but internally, doubt tugged at her. Not about Sam; she felt the same way about meeting him. She was the one who had gotten lucky. What she doubted was the odds of finding who that present belonged to.

Bunny wasn't one to give up easily, but for the first time, she had to admit she wasn't one hundred percent sure they'd be successful at solving this mystery.

# CHAPTER NINETEEN

Inside the animal rescue charity tent, Claire looked at her watch impatiently. She'd only been here an hour and had worked up a sweat dealing with a steady stream of people all by herself. Sandee was supposed to be here, too, not that Claire really wanted to spend time with her, but the woman had never shown up! She should not have been surprised.

The tent was a burst of autumnal colors set up near the sidewalks of Main Street. Under the canopy, tables were neatly arranged and covered with cheerful tablecloths that showcased falling leaves and pumpkins. In the middle of one table sat a donation jar, surrounded by an array of pet-themed trinkets—everything from little paw-print keychains to doggy bandanas. Another table was laden with baked goodies, among which Claire's own Beach Bones dog treats prominently stood out in their festive packaging. She'd brought them along and had pictured them competing side-by-side with Sandee's. At least that was one benefit to the other woman not showing up.

Claire bustled about, adjusting displays and greeting passersby with an enthusiasm that belied her annoyance. The tent was located perfectly to capture the afternoon sun, which cast a warm, inviting glow over everything. The weather was splendid—mild with a slight breeze, the kind of day that made her forget winter was just around the corner.

As people meandered down Main Street, the town's commitment to festive décor was evident everywhere. Twinkle lights adorned the shop fronts, each trying to outdo the next with an eye-catching arrangement of hay bales, scarecrows, and vibrantly colored mums. The paper luminaries, set up by locals earlier, outlined the pathways and seemed to invite evening to fall so they could show off their glow.

Claire glanced down the street to see Jane hurtling towards her. She entered the tent, a frown creasing her forehead as her eyes swept over the space.

"Hey, Claire! Wow, this all looks amazing," Jane exclaimed, but her tone carried a note of concern.

"Thanks. What's wrong?" Claire was genuinely

pleased to see her friend but sensed something was bothering Jane.

"Well, I came because I thought you might need some moral support." Jane glanced under a table then lowered her voice. "Where is she?"

Just then, Maxi burst into the tent, a little breathless but smiling broadly. "Hi, guys!"

"Maxi! I thought you'd be busy down at the art gallery. Did you find an artist?" Claire asked.

Maxi sighed. "No, but I needed to take a break and thought I'd stop by and—"

"Hidey-hoo, everyone," Andie's voice rang out from the side of the tent.

"It's getting a bit crowded in here." Claire smiled at her friends. "But in a good way."

"Claire, this is impressive, but where's Sandee? Wasn't she supposed to help?" Andie asked, and her eyes grew wide. "Oh no, what have you done with her?"

Claire laughed at the joke. "She was supposed to be here, but she never showed up. I should have known better."

"That's outrageous," Maxi said. "You can't do this all by yourself!"

"Actually, Marie was supposed to come by later, but she's tied up. She's coordinating relief for animal shelters in New York City that were affected by the floods," Claire explained, frustration and worry mixing in her voice. "She's stretched thin, and I don't want to add to her stress. But yes, Sandee not showing up didn't help."

"Wow, who skips out on a charity thing? That's really low," Jane said.

Claire paused for a moment, taking in the love and support she felt from her friends. It made her reflect on the tentative plans she'd had concerning Sandee. "You know, I was actually contemplating calling a truce with Sandee over the whole Beach Bones name debacle," she confessed.

"You were?" Maxi asked, a little surprised.

"Yeah. Tammi almost had me convinced that maybe I was wrong about Sandee. That perhaps she had good intentions and it was all a big misunderstanding," Claire explained, glancing at the assorted Beach Bones dog treats neatly arranged on a table.

"But her not showing up today..." Maxi trailed off, letting Claire finish the thought.

Claire shook her head, her expression resolute. "Exactly. It's like she's shown her true colors. I was willing to give her the benefit of the doubt, but not now. There's no way I'm letting her use the Beach Bones name."

"You go!" Andie turned around to look at the people who had gathered to look at the various items for sale. "Now, let's roll up our sleeves and help these people out."

Maxi stuffed her tote bag under the table. "What can we do to help?"

"Yeah, consider us your unofficial volunteers for the day," Jane added.

Claire looked at her friends, and her tension seemed to melt away. "You guys are amazing. Thank you so much."

# CHAPTER TWENTY

R ain hammered against Sandee's oversized raincoat as she tried to find a dry spot under the makeshift tarp. The chilling droplets trickled down her face, mingling with strands of hair glued to her forehead. Daniel, the rescue coordinator, looked over at her.

"We were severely short-staffed today. Your help made a world of difference. We saved more pets because of you," he said, his voice tinged with genuine appreciation. "Everything okay?" he asked, sensing her distant gaze.

Smiling, Sandee nodded. "Yes, everything's fine."

As Daniel turned his attention back to the rescued animals, Sandee's thoughts drifted to Lobster Bay. She felt a pang of guilt tighten in her chest. She'd promised to be at the charity tent for Prelude, and she felt guilty that she'd had to miss it. Marie had assured her over the phone that whoever was handling the tent could manage on their own, and her time was more needed here in the chaos of flood-hit New York City, yet the feeling of having let people down back in Lobster Bay was hard to shake.

Sandee and Daniel moved through the maze of makeshift kennels, both of them drenched but focused. Volunteers were milling about, each attending to an array of rescued animals—cats, dogs, even a couple of birds. In a large, waterlogged tent, several wash stations had been set up for cleaning the animals. Muffled barks and meows filled the air, a chaotic symphony of need.

Daniel looked around, clutching a clipboard. "We've got another twenty incoming. Foster families are maxed out."

Sandee paused, her eyes scanning the wet, shivering forms. "How many do we still need to place?"

"Eight, maybe more," Daniel said, flipping through his papers. His eyes met Sandee's, both understanding the gravity of their task.

Wordlessly, they divided their efforts. Sandee moved toward the wash stations where several dogs were tethered, waiting to be cleaned. She picked up a hose and started with a scruffy terrier mix, working the soap through its matted fur. Beside her, Daniel was doing the same with a trembling poodle. Other volunteers joined them, creating a sort of assembly line of washing, rinsing, and drying.

Once the dogs were clean, Sandee moved to the next station, where volunteers were checking each animal for identification tags or chips. "Any luck?" she asked a woman who was holding a scanner.

"A few. Maybe we can reunite them with their owners," the woman replied, hope lifting her voice.

Two hours passed like this, the work monotonous but deeply urgent. Sandee's muscles ached, her focus narrowed to the immediate needs before her. It was a type of tunnel vision that she welcomed, a state in which she could feel herself making a tangible difference, one animal at a time.

Finally, Daniel approached her. "We're running out of room, Sandee. I don't know where we're going to put the next batch."

"We need more transport out of the city," Sandee replied, already considering her options.

"I know, I know." Daniel sighed. "We've already sent some with Janine. Can you take any?"

Sandee considered for a moment. "I can take five. My car's not huge, but it's spacious enough."

"Five might be a lot for one person to handle," Daniel warned, clearly concerned. "And we already sent ten up to Marie in the van earlier. I think the shelter up there might be full."

"I can manage," Sandee insisted. "I'll keep any overflow dogs that don't find foster families at my house."

Convinced, Daniel led her to a group of five dogs, each different in size and breed but similar in their expressions of anxious hope. Sandee recognized the dalmatian mix she'd washed earlier and a stout bulldog with an underbite. She also saw a lanky greyhound and a German shepherd that had been keeping a watchful eye on everything.

Together, she and Daniel loaded the dogs into crates in Sandee's car. The greyhound seemed to fold into itself to fit into its crate, while the dalmatian whined softly, as if asking for reassurance. Sandee felt her heart swell and constrict, a curious mix of joy and pain.

The last to board was a tiny Chihuahua they'd just rescued. Shivering and wet, it looked up with large, vulnerable eyes as Daniel carefully placed it in a crate. "That's the last of them," he said, sliding the crated Chihuahua into the passenger seat.

Sandee looked at her car, now filled with the

anxious, hopeful faces of her charges. It was a heavy responsibility, but as she met each pair of eyes, she felt an inexplicable lightness, a sense of purpose that made every challenge seem trivial.

"Have a safe trip back, Sandee," Daniel said, closing the hatch.

She got into the driver's seat, her eyes meeting those of the assembled canines in her rearview mirror. As she started the engine, the vibrations seemed to offer a bit of comfort to the motley crew in the back, settling them down.

But it was the Chihuahua in the passenger seat that caught her attention. With a simple, heartfelt lick to her hand, the dog seemed to convey a universe of thanks and trust. When he looked up at her, his eyes were full of a love and gratitude so profound that it pierced right through her earlier reservations.

"Don't worry, buddy. We'll find your family," Sandee promised.

As she pulled out onto the rain-soaked road, that simple exchange dissolved any remaining fragments of doubt or guilt. Despite the challenges and the missed commitments, this—this right here—made it all worthwhile. With a newfound sense of resolve, Sandee began the long drive back to Lobster Bay, her heart full and her spirit lifted.

## CHAPTER TWENTY-ONE

The buzz of the oven timer cut through Bunny's concentration, momentarily diverting her attention from the endless scrolls of vintage Christmas wrapping paper displayed on her computer screen. She'd been squinting at these festive designs for hours, trying to pin down the exact year of that mysterious gift Andie had found. But so far, the origin of that beautifully wrapped box remained a tantalizing enigma.

Grateful for the interruption, Bunny stood up and made her way to the oven, where the scents of carrot, cinnamon, and nutmeg mixed harmoniously and made her mouth water.

She grabbed the floral oven mitt hanging from a hook near the stove, its fabric slightly faded from years of use but still fully functional. Sliding her hand into the mitt, she felt the quilted padding envelop her fingers as she opened the oven door. A wave of heat rolled out, warming her face and fogging up her glasses.

Carefully, she pulled out the muffin tin, each cavity filled with a perfectly risen carrot muffin, their tops golden brown. She set the tin on a wire rack to cool, inhaling deeply as another wave of that heavenly scent filled the air.

Bunny counted out a few muffins and set them aside on a small plate. Maxi would be arriving in about twenty minutes for her art lesson, and these muffins would make a perfect snack during their painting session. The rest she placed in a woven basket, covering them with a blue-and-white-checked cloth. Those were for Olga Svenson across the street.

Bunny picked up the basket and went out the front door. Leaves swirled around her doorstep, and she made a note to rake tomorrow. Everyone in the neighborhood liked to keep their lawns nicely maintained, and Bunny was no different. She loved the street with its large lots, abundance of trees, and blend of architectural styles and always did her part to keep it looking neat.

As she made her way across the street toward

Olga's quaint little house, she felt a sense of gratitude for this peaceful neighborhood. Here, looking out for one another was just a way of life, and Olga, with her years of wisdom and kindness, was a cherished part of that community fabric. Bunny was happy to be able to bring some muffins and have a nice chat with her neighbor. She'd been so busy with the investigation into the mysterious gift that she hadn't had time to talk to Olga in the past few days and wanted to catch up.

Bunny tapped lightly on the door and shifted the basket to her other arm as she waited for Olga to answer. The door creaked open, and there stood Olga, phone cradled between her ear and shoulder. She flashed a warm smile and gestured for Bunny to come inside.

Trying to be as discreet as possible, Bunny stepped into Olga's living room. As usual, the home was immaculate. The Danish modern furniture looked like it had just been cleaned. Gorgeous vases and boxes with colorful rosemaling—the flowering Scandinavian decorative folk painting—accented the room. Nothing appeared cluttered or out of place. Family photos adorned the walls, and a faint scent of potpourri filled the air.

Olga continued speaking into the phone, her face a mix of exasperation and resolve. "Yes, Richard, I've told you, I'm perfectly fine on my own," she said, firmly yet lovingly. "No, you and Kristina don't need to have someone looking in on me. I haven't burned the house down or forgotten my own name, have I? And besides, my neighbors take very good care of me." Olga smiled at Bunny.

Finally, Olga said her goodbyes and set the phone back in its cradle. "That was Richard," she sighed, shaking her head. "My son and daughter are ganging up on me again with this assisted-living nonsense. I swear, I don't know what I've done to make them think I can't manage on my own anymore."

Waving her hand dismissively, Olga shifted her focus to Bunny's basket. "But that's not your problem, dear," she said, her eyes lighting up as she peeked under the blue-and-white-checked cloth. "Oh, carrot muffins! You really shouldn't have, but I'm so glad you did."

Olga moved toward the kitchen. "I'll put on some tea, and we can enjoy these in the sunroom. The late-afternoon sun is lovely today," she announced, already reaching for the teapot.

Bunny walked toward the sunroom, a destination she had visited countless times during her trips to Olga's. But when she reached the doorway, she stopped dead in her tracks. Unlike the rest of Olga's neatly maintained house, the sunroom looked like a Scandinavian Christmas jumble sale.

Piles of items filled the space haphazardly. Dala horses were stacked on one side, their vibrant red and blue colors jumbled together in a kaleidoscopic heap. Tomtes, those gnome-like figures with their iconic pointed hats, were piled in a corner, no longer standing guard over anything specific but instead appearing to have congregated for a meeting of the mythical minds. Intricately carved wooden ornaments were heaped in baskets, their delicate craftsmanship hidden away under layers of other items. Boxes filled with slender Swedish Christmas trees, unassembled and packed away, were stacked against another wall.

Despite the disarray, the scent of traditional holiday spices—cardamom, cinnamon, perhaps a hint of cloves—still filled the air. The room seemed to have captured the spirit of the season in a wild, unorganized manner, as if it were a storage unit for cherished memories and beloved traditions that couldn't be contained.

Bunny moved to one of the wicker settees, pushing aside a cluster of embroidered Christmas pillows to make room. Then, she turned her attention to the small wicker table in front of where she was sitting. It was already covered with knickknacks: delicate straw ornaments, tiny advent calendars, and a scattering of Christmas cards. Carefully, she shifted these items to the edges, clearing a central space in which she placed the basket of freshly baked muffins.

Just then, Olga walked into the sunroom holding a tray laden with teacups, a pot of steaming tea, and various accompaniments like sugar cubes and lemon wedges. "Oh, my! Look at this mess," she exclaimed, setting down the tray, her eyes widening as they took in the room's cluttered state. "I apologize, Bunny. I normally wouldn't let anyone see the room like this."

"No need to apologize," Bunny assured her. "I think it's wonderful that you're so involved in your traditions."

Olga poured the tea, her hands slightly trembling but still remarkably steady for her age. The amber liquid flowed into the fine china cups, releasing a comforting aroma that mingled with the scent of Bunny's muffins. "Ah, traditions. Yes, they keep us grounded, don't they?"

With a soft clink, she placed the teapot back on the tray and then picked up her cup. "You see, I've been making these decorations and delivering them all over town. I've spent hours decorating Tall Pines Retirement Home. I even sent a batch of ornaments with Liz over to Tides Inn."

Bunny listened intently, sipping her tea and taking a bite of a carrot muffin.

"It's really been consuming all my time, but I don't mind," Olga continued. "Do you know why? Because it's my little act of rebellion. My children, bless their hearts, have been urging me to move into assisted living. But what they don't understand is that I'm perfectly capable of living on my own."

Olga's eyes gleamed with a mix of defiance and sorrow. "This," she gestured broadly at the piles of Scandinavian Christmas artifacts surrounding them, "is my proof of life, so to speak. I want to show them that I'm not just some helpless old lady who needs constant watching. I'm active, involved in my community, and committed to my traditions. I'm still the mother who taught them the importance of heritage, the value of community, and the magic of Christmas."

Bunny felt her eyes moisten. She reached over and touched Olga's hand. "Olga, you don't have to prove anything to anyone. You're amazing just as you are."

Olga smiled, her eyes twinkling like the Christmas lights that she'd no doubt hung herself. "Well, sometimes, we do have to remind people, even our own children, who we really are. I hope they will come to see I'm fine on my own, though I do think I need something more, something bigger, perhaps."

As they sat there, sipping their tea and discussing everything from the upcoming Lobster Bay holiday festivities to the current book Olga was reading, Bunny couldn't shake what Olga had shared earlier. Her words resonated in Bunny's mind like a haunting melody—needing something big to prove to her own children that she was just fine on her own. Bunny wished she could help Olga, but how?

# CHAPTER TWENTY-TWO

laire's phone buzzed on the folding table next to a stack of "Adopt, Don't Shop" flyers. She glanced at the screen and saw Marie's name. "Excuse me, I have to take this," she told Andie, Maxi, and Jane as she stepped away.

"Marie, what's up?"

"Five dogs are coming up from New York," Marie reported, her voice tinged with urgency. "We need fosters. Are you still up for it?"

Claire hesitated, thinking of her territorial cat, Whiskers. "I can't, Marie. My cat would have a fit. But Rob Bradford said he'd be willing to foster one."

"Wonderful! If you know of anyone else who will foster, let me know. Thanks, Claire."

Hanging up, Claire rejoined the group, who were

sorting through some donations. "That was Marie. Five dogs need fostering because of the flooding in New York."

Jane looked up from a box of leashes. "Are you taking one?"

Claire shook her head. "No, but Rob is."

Maxi grinned mischievously. "Rob's spending so much time at your place, you might as well be taking one."

Claire felt her cheeks warm. "What? Are you guys stalking me?"

Maxi rolled her eyes. "Nope. It's obvious."

Jane looked up from the box of leashes she was sorting through. "That's great that Rob is doing that. I know a foster is only temporary, but having Cooper has really enriched my life. Dogs just bring so much joy."

Claire cast a playful glance at Jane. "Having Mike around seems to have had a similar effect on you."

Jane's face flushed a delightful shade of pink, and her eyes sparkled with happiness. "Well, I can't argue with that."

Claire glanced up from the donation jar as a rush of fresh air swept into the tent, heralding the arrival of four women loaded with shopping bags expertly balanced in their arms.

"Jane!" one of them said.

Jane turned, and her eyes lit up in recognition. "Everyone, meet Carol, Susan, Betty, and Margie. They're staying at Tides. Ladies, these are my dear friends—Claire and Maxi, and you already know my sister, Andie."

Pleasantries and handshakes were exchanged, filling the tent with a warm camaraderie.

"So lovely to meet you all," Claire said, gesturing toward the table filled with pet-themed trinkets. "This is the animal rescue charity tent, in case you didn't notice. Proceeds go to our local animal rescue."

"Oh, I love animals! I have a Bichon Frisé named Charlie." Susan beamed, her eyes sparkling as she started to describe her pet. "He's the most curious little guy—has a knack for stealing socks. You'll find him hoarding them under the bed like they're pure gold!"

Betty chuckled at Susan's story before chiming in. "And you should meet my dachshund, Oliver. He's quite the entertainer. Whenever I play the piano, he howls along as if he's providing the backup vocals. He's the Pavarotti of the dog world!"

Laughter rippled through the tent at Betty's vivid description.

"They both sound utterly adorable," Claire remarked, genuinely charmed by their stories.

"And worthy causes like this are so close to our hearts because of them," Susan said, pulling out a bill from her purse and dropping it into the donation jar.

Betty followed suit, her charm bracelet jingling as her hand reached into her stylish tote to retrieve her wallet, from which she pulled another generous bill.

Carol and Margie followed suit with generous donations.

"Thank you all so much. Every bit helps," Claire gratefully acknowledged.

"Jane mentioned that you four come back every year," Maxi said.

Margie nodded. "We love coming back to Lobster Bay for Prelude and some preholiday shopping. Of course, we love doing our favorite things, too, like the Marginal Way, and we're about to head to the Rachel Carson Preserve to watch for deer."

"The preserve is magical this time of year," Maxi observed, her eyes lighting up at the mention.

"And afterward, we have a reservation at Oarweeds," Susan said.

"I love their clam chowder," Claire said.

"Me too," Margie agreed.

"We may be living all over the place now—Boston, Denver, San Francisco, and Atlanta—but Lobster Bay remains our common bond," Betty declared, her voice tinged with nostalgia.

Nods and smiles of agreement circled around the tent.

"Well, we better get a move on," Susan secured her bag on her arm. "Hope to see you all around town!"

Claire watched as Carol, Susan, Margie, and Betty disappeared into the festively decorated main street, their laughter fading into the distant sound of carolers.

"They seem like really nice guests," Maxi commented, her gaze following their figures until they vanished from view.

Jane smiled in agreement. "Oh, they are. A pleasure to have breakfast with—always full of stories and laughter, though Betty seems a little sad."

"I did sense that. I wonder why," Claire asked.

"She mentioned losing her sister when they were kids, and coming back probably brings up bittersweet memories." Jane glanced at Andie, and Claire's heart swooped at the affection between the two sisters.

"That's sad," Andie said, putting her arm around Jane.

"It is." Maxi glanced at her watch, and her eyes widened. "Oh, I have to go. I've got an art lesson with Bunny!"

Claire gave her a hug. "You better get going, then. Thanks so much for your help!"

Andie chimed in with, "Hope you find that perfect client for your gallery. Your event will be amazing, I'm sure of it."

Jane added her own sentiments. "Yeah, the universe has a way of working these things out, especially around the holidays."

"Thank you all. That means the world to me. See you soon!"

With a wave, Maxi left the tent. Claire, Andie, and Jane watched her go, each privately sending good wishes her way.

# CHAPTER TWENTY-THREE

Maxi pulled up in front of Bunny's charming home and admired the small white pumpkins Bunny had lined up on her porch. The neighborhood was a postcard of fall décor, with mums and pumpkins adorning each front porch and yard.

Walking up to the door, she took a moment to appreciate Bunny's seasonal touches. A wreath made of autumn leaves hung on the front door, and planters with mums in various colors were arranged artfully on the steps.

Bunny welcomed Maxi in, the warm aroma of fresh-baked carrot muffins filling the air.

"Wow, it smells heavenly in here," Maxi said, her eyes widening at the sight of the golden-brown muffins on the kitchen counter.

"Thank you! I figured we could use something homemade when we take a break from painting," Bunny said, leading Maxi to the back room where easels and paints were set up, ready for their artistic endeavors.

The room was awash in late-afternoon light, illuminating the paint palettes and brushes that lay on a table near the easels. Through the glass patio doors, they could see Liz Weston in the garden, busy harvesting the last of the pumpkins.

"Now, today's lesson is highlights. I know you've been wanting to improve in that area," Bunny said, gesturing to the easels and the beautiful outdoor tableau beyond.

"I sure have." Maxi picked up a brush and palette. The paints were all laid out, and she soon got to work on an ocean scene, with Bunny closely watching.

Maxi dipped her brush into the dollop of titanium white, her fingers tingling with a mix of anticipation and apprehension. Highlights. They always seemed to elude her, either too stark or too subtle, never capturing the natural shimmer she aimed for.

"Remember, Maxi, less is often more when it comes to highlights," Bunny said, her voice as soothing as a warm cup of tea. "You want to think about where the light source is in your painting. Place your high-lights accordingly."

Maxi glanced at her canvas. It was a seascape today, a vivid sunset stretching across the sky and cascading its fiery hues onto the rippling water below. She touched the brush lightly to the crest of a wave.

"That's it," Bunny encouraged. "A light touch. Just kiss the canvas with the brush."

Heart buoyed by Bunny's assurance, Maxi added more glints to the wave tips, her brush dancing across the canvas as if guided by an unseen hand. A sense of awe washed over her; the canvas seemed to glow with newfound life, the highlights transforming flat shapes into voluminous forms.

She took a step back, amazed at how such small strokes could bring out such immense depth and emotion. A satisfied smile spread across her face, mirrored by Bunny's own beam.

"You've got it, Maxi. Those highlights are just what this painting needed to come alive."

Maxi's chest swelled with pride. This was a skill she'd long struggled with, but now, thanks to Bunny's expert guidance, she felt she'd crossed an important threshold.

"I think now would be a great time for a break," Bunny said.

"Good. I'm starving." Maxi carefully placed her paintbrush in the jar of turpentine, her thoughts still swirling around the artistic breakthrough she'd just experienced.

Bunny led the way to the kitchen. "Tea and muffins, the perfect artist's break," Bunny said as she popped the muffins into the oven to heat and put on water for tea. Five minutes later, Maxi had a warm muffin and a cup of Earl Grey in front of her.

Maxi eagerly slathered butter over the muffin, the melted goodness soaking into the crumbly top. The first bite was heavenly, a sweet and nutty flavor that seemed to encapsulate all the cozy comfort of a home kitchen.

"So, how's the mystery solving going?" Maxi asked, catching Bunny's gaze.

Bunny sighed, her shoulders drooping a little. "I wish I could say I've cracked it wide open, but it's more like I've just scratched the surface. Andie's mystery has proven more elusive than I'd hoped. What about you?" Bunny asked, shifting the topic. "The gallery's big reveal is in two days, right? How's that going?"

Maxi grimaced. "It's stressful. The criteria are very specific. We're looking for something that's holiday themed but also carries a cultural element. And I can't find anyone who fits the bill."

Bunny's eyes twinkled, a spark of inspiration crossing her face. "Does it have to be paintings?"

"No, not at all. Any form of art would work," Maxi said.

"So handmade art would be considered?"

"Handmade would be perfect," Maxi assured her.

Bunny looked out the kitchen window, her gaze falling on Olga Svenson's house across the street. A knowing smile crept onto her lips.

"Come on," Bunny said, rising from her chair. "I think I have an idea that might just solve two problems."

# CHAPTER TWENTY-FOUR

Betty sat in the back seat of the car they'd rented for a few days, her eyes tracing the path of oak leaves as they swirled in the air and gently landed on the road. Susan's hands were steady on the wheel, guiding them down the oak-lined lane leading to the Rachel Carson Preserve. It was dusk, that magical time when the world seemed to pause, holding its breath in anticipation of the night.

Carol and Margie filled the car with laughter and stories from their trip, the camaraderie warming the air. "This has been such a fantastic getaway," Carol said, looking back at Betty through the rearview mirror. "I couldn't have asked for better company."

"Absolutely," Margie agreed, her eyes scanning the

large field that bordered the road. "The shopping, the food, and now the nature—this trip has had it all."

"I couldn't agree more," Susan added, adjusting the rearview mirror slightly. "I can't remember the last time I felt this relaxed."

Betty nodded, her smile genuine but tinged with an inner weight. "It's been amazing, truly."

Betty felt a tug of mixed emotions. She had enjoyed every bit of this trip—the laughter, the bonding, the new memories—but underneath it all, the memory of her sister lurked. Whenever she visited places of natural beauty like this, the thought of her sister was never far away. Their family had come here many times, and Betty still remembered sitting in the back seat with her sister. At least now those memories brought a smile to her face.

Suddenly, Margie let out a soft gasp, her finger pointing toward the edge of the field. "Look, there they are!"

A small group of deer had emerged from the woods, their silhouettes framed by the dimming light. For a moment, the car fell silent, all four women captivated by the peaceful creatures grazing at the field's edge.

In that silent space, Betty's heart held a quiet wish —a longing, really—that one of the deer would venture closer, right up to their car. It was a silly thought, one born from the depths of her hope and imagination. She had always envisioned such an event as a sign, a small cosmic signal from her sister that she was still with her in spirit.

But the deer stayed where they were, peacefully nibbling at the grass, as if understanding the sacred boundary between humans and nature.

Finally, Susan broke the silence. "This moment— it's like the perfect bow on top of our trip."

"Agreed," Carol murmured, her eyes still fixed on the deer.

Margie snapped a few pictures, her face glowing with awe. "I can't wait to share these."

Betty smiled, appreciating the beauty of the moment even if it hadn't fulfilled her quiet, private hope. "It's perfect," she said softly, wrapping up her complex swirl of emotions in those two simple words. The trip had been wonderful, and the sight of the deer felt like a fitting end, even if the secret yearning of her heart remained unmet. As they drove away, she took one last look at the field, committing the serene scene to memory.

## CHAPTER TWENTY-FIVE

**B**unny nibbled at the last of her carrot muffin, her eyes scanning the crossword grid in front of her. She had just filled in the last box, completing the puzzle. A sense of accomplishment washed over her, because it wasn't just the crossword she had conquered today. Maxi's art lesson had been a success, and she may have solved a problem for two people.

"Now, if only I could solve this gift mystery," she mused.

Her thoughts were interrupted by the jingling melody of her phone. Glancing at the screen, she saw it was Sam.

"Hey, Sam, what's up?" she greeted him, the excitement already building in her voice.

"Bunny, you won't believe what I found!" His

voice crackled with enthusiasm. "I was at the library, going through some old church bulletins, and guess what? I think I've found a clue about our Christmas gift mystery."

"Do tell!" she urged.

Sam read out a line from one of the bulletins, dated back to one of the years they had suspected the present could be from. "Listen to this: 'To the family who has put the holidays on hold, may you find your Christmas spirit again.'"

Bunny's heart skipped a beat. "That could explain the undelivered gift! A family that didn't celebrate Christmas that year for some reason might have forgotten about a hidden present."

"Exactly," Sam concurred. "I think we should dive deeper into these church bulletins. Maybe we can figure out why they didn't celebrate Christmas that year. We could even talk to Father Frank."

"Sounds like a plan. Meet you downtown?"

"Sure, in about thirty minutes?"

"Perfect. Oh, and by the way, I finished the crossword. I win our little challenge," Bunny gloated, unable to suppress a chuckle.

Laughing, Sam replied, "You always do, don't you? See you soon."

After hanging up, Bunny grabbed her keys,

slipped on her coat, and headed out to her car. The engine roared to life, and she took the familiar route downtown, her thoughts racing ahead of her. As she pulled into a parking spot, she glanced around. The area was buzzing with activity; it was dusk, and the twinkling streetlights cast a magical glow. The small village was loaded with tourists, and everyone seemed to be enjoying the magic of Lobster Bay Prelude.

She peeked down the street where Maxi's art gallery was located. Through the paper-covered windows, she could see shadows moving about and lights flickering on. *Good*, she thought. *Looks like things are coming together for the big reveal.*

Now, if she could just solve the mystery of the undelivered present.

Bunny spotted Andie and Shane walking toward her. Her eyes instantly lit up, and she couldn't wait to tell Andie that they might be on to something.

"Hey, you two. Don't you look cozy." Bunny was glad to see the couple so happy together.

"Thanks. We are." Shane put his arm around Andie's waist and squeezed. Andie beamed.

"How's the Crosby job coming along?" Shane was retired from the Navy and now a carpenter who specialized in additions around town. He'd built quite a business for himself and was doing a kitchen renovation at one of Bunny's friends' houses.

"We're making good progress. Should wrap up just in time for their family Christmas," Shane responded, a pleased smile gracing his face.

"How's the investigation going?" Andie asked.

"I thought you'd never ask," Bunny teased. "Sam might be on to something. In fact, I'm heading to the library to meet him."

"Really? Do tell!" Andie's eyes sparkled with keen interest, reflecting her impatience to hear the details.

Bunny quickly spilled the beans about the church bulletin Sam had discovered, about the family that had "put the holidays on hold," and their plans to delve deeper into the church archives.

"That's amazing! It sounds like you're getting close!" Andie said, visibly thrilled.

"As promising as that lead sounds," Shane added, his tone tempered with a touch of caution, "don't forget the present is really old, and there weren't many clues in the trunk to begin with. It might still be impossible to figure out exactly where it came from."

Bunny nodded, acknowledging the note of caution in Shane's words. "You're right, of course. But we've got to follow every lead we have, no matter how slim the chances."

"Absolutely," Shane agreed, his eyes meeting hers in a reassuring gaze. "But sometimes, mysteries are part of the magic, too."

"True, but either way, it keeps Sam and me exercising our gray matter, so it's all good." Bunny gave them each a pat on the arm. "Well, I better be on my way—Sam's waiting. Nice to see you both!"

# CHAPTER TWENTY-SIX

M axi couldn't believe her eyes as she looked around the gallery space. They'd loaded all of Olga's items into her car and raced over to the gallery. In less than two hours, Olga had transformed it into a Scandinavian Christmas wonderland, brimming with handcrafted items that told stories of a culture deeply rooted in tradition and festivity. There were intricately knitted julekuler ornaments, their patterns reflecting age-old Nordic designs, soon to hang on a faux Christmas tree at the center of the room. Hand-carved dala horses and small wooden figurines of tomte, the little Swedish gnome, were laid out on a table, ready for placement on shelves.

Along the walls, Olga had spread out yards of

beautifully embroidered linen and colorful woven jul runners. A delicate mobile featuring the St. Lucia procession, crafted from thin sheets of birch, was yet to be suspended from the ceiling, promising to add an ethereal quality to the space. Candleholders designed in the unique kurbits style often seen in Swedish folk art were being positioned on the counter next to an arrangement of traditional woven heart baskets.

As they moved around, placing each item with care and intention, Maxi finally broke the silence. "Olga, I can't even begin to express my gratitude. This is beyond amazing. I hope it's not too much for you, though."

Olga waved away Maxi's concerns with an energetic hand. "Oh, don't you worry about me, young lady. I'm a lot spryer than people give me credit for—especially my children." A wistful expression crossed her face. "Hopefully, this will prove to them, once and for all, that their old mother can manage just fine on her own. They don't have to fuss so much."

"If this doesn't convince them, I don't know what will," Maxi replied, genuinely impressed. "Pulling off a one-woman art show like this is no small feat."

Olga's eyes twinkled as she looked at Maxi. "Well, they always say experience comes with age, and I've had plenty of both."

Maxi took a step back, looking at the gallery from a variety of angles. It looked fantastic. Chandler would be impressed.

"You know, we have Bunny to thank for this incredible collaboration," Maxi said, smiling at the thought of how Bunny had brought them together.

Olga adjusted one of the displays. "Ah, yes, Bunny. She's such a nice lady. Quick thinker too."

Maxi nodded. "And makes great carrot muffins."

"Indeed." Olga smiled.

"The moment I saw your Scandinavian pieces, I knew they'd be perfect for the gallery. They capture the essence of the holidays while offering something unique and deeply cultural."

"Ah, you flatter me," Olga said, beaming. "I was so thrilled when Bunny suggested the idea. It's a wonderful opportunity to showcase a part of my heritage that's so dear to me."

Maxi couldn't help but ask, "You've created so many pieces, Olga. Where does all this energy and ambition come from?"

Olga chuckled. "Well, you know, dear, age hasn't sapped my enthusiasm for life. Crafting these pieces is a hobby that brings me immense joy. And let's just say I still have a wellspring of energy and a backlog of ideas."

"It's evident in every piece," Maxi agreed. "But what did you plan to do with all of these beautiful items before the gallery idea came up?"

Olga laughed heartily. "Oh, you won't believe it, but I was running out of people to gift them to! My home started looking like a Scandinavian holiday market. It's a good thing you found a purpose for them; otherwise, my children would have had another reason to fuss over me—'Mom's hoarding Christmas decorations again!'"

Maxi laughed along with Olga, but as her eyes scanned the room, her gaze caught on the bare walls. The thought escaped her lips before she could filter it. "The walls, though...they're so empty."

Olga chuckled. "Ah, you're right. But don't you worry about that either. I can paint some rosemaling artwork to fill those spaces. It's a traditional Norwegian decorative painting, you see. Perfect for our theme here!"

"Rosemaling?" Maxi's eyes lit up as she pictured canvases filled with the colorful folk art on the walls. "That sounds fantastic, but again, don't push yourself too hard."

"Pushing ourselves is how we grow, dear," Olga said, her eyes twinkling mischievously. "Besides, how else will I convince my overprotective children that their mom can still function on her own and still has a lot of life in her?"

Maxi laughed, grateful for Olga's wisdom and resilience. "Well, if this gallery showing doesn't prove it, I don't know what will."

# CHAPTER TWENTY-SEVEN

As the evening sun dipped below the horizon, Claire and Rob found themselves pulling into the parking lot of a somewhat rundown apartment complex. The building had seen better days, and Claire couldn't help but wonder if they were in the right place.

"Are you sure you want to foster a dog? I hope I didn't push you into this," Claire said, eyeing the tired facade of the building as Rob parked the car.

Rob looked at her, smiling as he placed his hand reassuringly over hers. "Not at all. I'm actually pretty excited about it. But are you sure this is the right place?"

Claire double-checked the address that Marie had texted her earlier. "Yes, this is it."

Claire rang the doorbell, feeling the evening chill seep through her jacket. The door swung open, and her jaw dropped. Standing on the other side was a woman Claire could scarcely recognize as Sandee—dressed in jeans and a dirty sweatshirt with her hair in disarray.

"You?" both women said almost simultaneously.

"You live here?" Claire asked, her eyebrows knitting together.

Sandee crossed her arms over her chest, defensive. "Yes. Peter and I have separated."

At that moment, a cacophony of barks and yips filled the air as a cluster of dogs scrambled about. Sandee smiled, crouching to pet them and hushing their noisy enthusiasm. She opened the door wider, inviting Claire and Rob inside.

Claire gestured toward Rob. "This is Rob."

"Yes, from the bread store," Sandee said, extending her hand to Rob.

Rob chuckled, "Yes, and I remember you like crusty French bread."

For a brief second, Claire felt a pang of jealousy. Was Sandee flirting with Rob? But she quickly reassured herself. She trusted Rob, and Sandee seemed more interested in the dogs than in Rob.

"You can take your pick." Sandee gestured to the dogs.

Rob scanned the excited faces and wagging tails before his eyes settled on the dalmatian mix. "How about him?"

"He's yours! But understand, we're trying to find the owners of these lost dogs," Sandee explained, petting the chosen dog affectionately. "If they've run off because they're scared, they might get separated from their families. So he might not be with you for long. But if we can't find his owner, you're more than welcome to adopt him, of course."

Rob seemed to mull this over as he petted the dog, clearly already enamored.

As Claire and Rob prepared to leave, she turned to Sandee. "By the way, I managed just fine at the animal rescue charity tent today."

For a fleeting moment, Sandee's eyes met Claire's, and she looked genuinely regretful. "I'm sorry I couldn't make it," she said, gesturing toward the whirl-wind of canine activity around them. "As you can see, I've been a bit tied up. Just got back, actually."

Claire's curiosity was piqued. Marie had mentioned something about a volunteer from their group going to New York City for an emergency rescue operation. She'd never imagined that Sandee,

163

who always seemed so wrapped up in herself, would do something so selfless.

"You went to New York?" Claire couldn't hide her surprise.

"Yes." Sandee nodded. "It was a last-minute thing. They needed all the help they could get."

Claire was momentarily taken aback. Perhaps there really was more to Sandee than met the eye. The thought was humbling and nudged at her preconceptions.

Claire wanted to say more, but the dog was already tugging Rob toward the door, and she wasn't even exactly sure what to say.

Claire and Rob returned to the car, the dog happily sitting in the back seat.

"Do you think you'll keep him if they don't find the owner?" Claire couldn't help but ask, noticing how Rob already treated the dog like a long-lost friend.

Rob sighed. "I don't know. It's tough. I'm worried about getting too attached and then having to give him up."

Claire chuckled. "Then don't name him!"

Rob looked puzzled. "But we have to call him something. Just calling him Dog doesn't seem right."

The conversation shifted as Rob looked over at Claire. "You know, I thought you said Sandee was all about appearances. Wearing designer clothes, always perfectly styled. But she seemed rather down-to-earth today," he noted, one hand resting on the steering wheel, the other patting the dog sitting behind them.

Claire bit her bottom lip, her mind reeling with the day's revelations. "She did, didn't she? I've always had this image of her, and today just didn't fit that mold. Maybe you're right. Maybe I've been seeing her in just one light. Tammi did say that people are complex, and maybe she's wiser than I give her credit for sometimes."

Rob nodded. "Tammi has a good head on her shoulders. It's easy to pigeonhole people based on a few interactions, but everyone has layers we don't see."

Claire sighed. "True. It's a lesson I keep learning. But you know what they say, 'A leopard doesn't change its spots,'" she added cautiously, still not fully ready to change her opinion about Sandee.

"Spot! That's a great name for him!" Rob exclaimed, his face lighting up as he turned to pet the dog again. "See, he likes it."

Claire chuckled, her heart warming at Rob's enthusiasm. "He does seem to be responding to it," she admitted.

Rob grinned. "It's settled, then. Spot it is, at least for now."

AFTER CLOSING the door behind Rob and Claire, Sandee collapsed on her worn-out couch, her muscles aching and her mind buzzing. She looked around at the whirlpool of wagging tails and excited eyes surrounding her. There was Bella, a golden retriever with a heart of gold, and Rosco, a lumbering, lovable mastiff. Dexter, the high-energy border collie, was already vying for her attention. And then there was Peanut, the tiny Chihuahua, who hid behind the larger dogs, trembling and clearly still frightened by all the recent changes.

She reached into a jar on the coffee table and pulled out some of her homemade red Beach Bones treats. "Okay, everyone, treat time!" she announced. The room erupted into happy barks. Even Peanut inched forward at the smell, his tiny nose twitching.

As she handed out the treats, her mind wandered back to Claire's unexpected appearance. She hadn't known Claire was dating Rob. The moment their eyes met, she'd seen something flicker in Claire's gaze—an inkling of understanding, maybe? As if Claire finally saw that Sandee wasn't the villain she'd painted her to be. And was that a hint of jealousy? Sandee had to admit, Rob was kind of cute. But the idea of encroaching on Claire's territory never crossed her mind, and besides, Sandee was done with men for the foreseeable future.

Her relationship with Peter had taught her the importance of focusing on herself, her own happiness, and these abandoned animals that gave her so much joy and purpose. "Right, guys?" she asked, scratching Bella's ears, earning a thump-thump of approval via the dog's wagging tail.

She thought about the uneasy truce between her and Claire. If there were ever a time for the ice to thaw, it seemed like now could be it. But Sandee wasn't going to make the first move. She'd extended the olive branch before, and it had snapped. This time, if Claire wanted peace—if she wanted to negotiate about Beach Bones—she'd have to be the one to extend her hand first.

And until then, Sandee had these wonderful dogs to keep her company. She sank deeper into her couch, allowing herself a rare moment to just breathe, each wagging tail and wet nose nudging her closer to something that felt like redemption. "We're a motley crew, but we're perfect," she whispered, smiling as even little Peanut finally hopped onto the couch, curling into a tiny ball beside her.

# CHAPTER TWENTY-EIGHT

The office of Father Frank at St. Mary's was as unassuming as the man himself—a room of simple, utilitarian design. A wooden desk, a couple of chairs, and a small bookshelf filled with theological texts and Bibles occupied the space. The walls were adorned only with a crucifix and a framed painting of the Virgin Mary. There were no frills, just essentials, and that seemed to perfectly match Father Frank.

Father Frank, the embodiment of pleasantness, sat across from them. He had a calming presence, eyes twinkling with an inherent kindness. Snow-white side-burns framed his lined face, complementing his genial appearance. His voice, gentle yet firm, had the unique ability to put anyone instantly at ease.

Internally, Bunny was practically buzzing with

excitement. She felt they were on the verge of solving the mystery of the gift and finally finding the intended recipient. She glanced at Sam, who looked equally expectant as he handed Father Frank the church bulletin they'd found.

After uncovering the bulletin that mentioned a family facing a joyless Christmas, Bunny and Sam had decided to delve deeper into the church archives. Their persistence had paid off when they stumbled upon another article that highlighted a charity benefit organized for a local family. The article went on to describe how the community had come together in an unprecedented manner, contributing record-breaking donations that included a sizable trunk brimming with gifts. The article didn't mention who the family was, but Bunny figured that if anyone would know, it would be Father Frank.

Father Frank took his reading glasses from his desk and skimmed through the pages. "Ah, I remember this well," he said, referring to the notice about the charity benefit and the trunk full of donated gifts. "I was just a young priest back then. We held a benefit for a family in dire straits. The father had died suddenly, leaving the wife and children to fend for themselves."

As they talked, Bunny couldn't shake off a nagging feeling. The notion of the gift being merely overlooked seemed too simple, too convenient. She looked over at Father Frank and Sam, feeling the weight of the unsolved mystery on her shoulders.

"But then, how did the trunk end up in Mrs. Perkins's attic?" Bunny asked, her eyebrows knitting together in confusion.

Father Frank paused, considering the question. "That is indeed puzzling. Perhaps the trunk was misplaced and then forgotten over the years. When families go through significant changes, especially under stressful circumstances, things can be easily misplaced or misattributed."

Sam nodded. "And then maybe when someone cleaned out the house, no one remembered what the trunk was for. It could've just gotten lumped in with everything else."

"That could be," Father Frank agreed. "Mrs. Quillen moved to Tall Pines a few years ago. She's almost ninety, you know. Before she moved, her children had a big estate sale. Maybe in the shuffle of selling off items and cleaning the house, the trunk found its way to Mrs. Perkins's attic."

"Mrs. Quillen? She's still alive?" Sam queried, eager to follow the trail.

Father Frank nodded. "Yes. Her name is Ellen. Her children have moved away, but she's still here and sharp as a tack, though she needs help with mobility."

Bunny's eyes widened, her excitement reaching a new peak. "Sounds like we need to go to Tall Pines. It's late tonight, but maybe we can take Andie and the gift tomorrow."

Father Frank's eyes twinkled even more brightly if that were possible. "It would truly be a holiday wonder to reunite the gift with its intended recipient."

As they stood up to leave, Father Frank offered a final blessing. "May your journey be filled with discovery and your hearts with fulfillment."

Bunny felt a wave of serenity wash over her, mingling with her excitement. She made a mental note to zip a text off to Andie and arrange a time. She couldn't wait for tomorrow.

# CHAPTER TWENTY-NINE

The next morning at Sandcastles, the café was a cozy hive of activity. The scent of freshly brewed coffee mingled with the aroma of cinnamon and sugar from the pastries cooling on wire racks. Claire and Hailey were in their element, moving seamlessly from the counter to the tables, their aprons filled with orders. A display of buttery croissants, crumbly blueberry scones, and decadent chocolate chip muffins beckoned to customers from behind the glass case.

Claire's spirits lifted even further when she saw Rob walk in, a cheerful expression on his face. Through the café's large window, she noticed Spot tied securely to a post. He was sitting obediently, his eyes keenly following Rob.

"Hey," Rob greeted as he approached the counter,

"just stopping by for my usual, and maybe a little something for Spot?"

While Hailey steamed the milk for Rob's latte, Claire couldn't help but ask, "How did Spot do on the way to the store? He was a lot of fun last night. I can tell someone trained him well."

"Yeah, he's a good boy." Rob glanced out at the dog. "He didn't mind the ride and is already acting like he owns the place even though he has to stay in the office."

Claire handed over Rob's latte, a small bag with the Beach Bones, and one of Rob's favorite pastries, a cheese danish. "The cat was a bit miffed when I went home to feed him this morning. I think he sensed that I've been spending time with another animal."

Rob chuckled. "Jealous, is he?"

"A bit." Claire laughed. "But he'll get over it."

The door chime jingled, and in walked Marie, dressed in her usual animal-themed attire. She looked around the café, spotted Rob, and headed straight for him.

"Rob, I wanted to thank you again for fostering that dog," Marie started, her eyes warm and appreciative.

"You mean Spot," Rob grinned, his eyes meeting

Claire's for a brief second. "I've decided to name him Spot."

"Spot, huh?" Marie chuckled. "Well, don't get too attached just yet. We're still trying to locate his owners."

"But if we don't?" Rob asked, raising an eyebrow.

Marie looked at Spot and then back to Rob and Claire, a twinkle in her eye. "If we don't, I have a strong feeling that Spot has already found himself a good home."

Claire couldn't help but smile at the thought. Then, switching gears, she turned to Marie and said, "Could I have Sandee's phone number?"

Rob looked puzzled but didn't say anything as Marie quickly scribbled down Sandee's number on a piece of paper and handed it over to Claire.

"Thanks, Marie," Claire said. "Would you like anything? A raspberry almond croissant? Or perhaps an apple-cinnamon scone?"

"You know, both sound delightful," Marie answered, pulling out her wallet. "One of each, please."

After ringing up Marie's order and watching her leave with a smile, Rob finally asked, "So, why'd you ask for Sandee's number?"

Claire sighed a little, gathering her thoughts. "I

think you and Tammi might be on to something. Maybe I've been too hard on her, misjudged her. Plus, the dogs seem to prefer her red Beach Bones biscuits, so it could be a smart business move."

Rob looked at Claire, his eyes glowing with pride and love. "That's my girl," he said, pushing his fist over the counter.

Claire bumped her fist to his and laughed. "We'll see how it works out."

"I think you might be surprised. Thanks for the coffee and pastry." Rob raised the bag and exited, stopping to untie Spot. As they trotted off, he looked back over his shoulder and gave her a wave.

Claire was still holding onto the piece of paper with Sandee's number when Hailey wandered over, drying her hands on a towel.

"Is that one of the fosters from the NYC run?" Hailey nodded toward Rob and Spot, who were still crossing the street.

"Yeah," Claire affirmed. "Did you know that Sandee went down to get them?"

Hailey's brows shot up in surprise. "Really? I have heard that she's gotten a lot nicer lately."

Claire rolled her eyes. "You too?"

Hailey laughed, her eyes twinkling. "Maybe she's turning over a new leaf or something."

Before Claire could reply, Hailey spotted a new customer walking through the door. 'I'll get them," she said, scurrying off to attend to the incoming patron.

Left with her thoughts, Claire found herself fiddling with the piece of paper. Taking a deep breath, she dialed Sandee's number. Her pulse quickened as the phone rang. "What if this is a disaster?" she thought.

Claire felt a momentary sense of relief when the call went to voicemail. "Hi, Sandee, it's Claire," she began, trying to keep her voice steady. "I was wondering if we could meet tomorrow morning at Sandcastles to discuss some business. Stop by around eight if you are interested. Thanks."

She hung up, placing her phone on the counter. Her feelings were a mixture of relief and tension. Sandee probably wouldn't even show, she reasoned with herself. But what if she did?

Claire looked up to see Bunny, Sam, and Andie walking toward the door. She picked up the bag of chocolate chip muffins and other pastries that she'd set aside for Andie to take to Tall Pines and pushed thoughts of Sandee out of her mind. Whatever would happen, she'd deal with it tomorrow.

# CHAPTER THIRTY

Andie clutched the Sandcastles bag in her hand as the trio entered Tall Pines. The place was a large complex with interconnected buildings that seemed more like a small community than an assisted-living facility. There were various rooms for the residents to watch TV or do a puzzle as well as a big dining room and several cafés.

Stopping at the reception desk, Bunny said, "We're here to visit Ellen Quillen. Could you please tell us where to find her?"

"Certainly," the receptionist replied with a welcoming smile. "Mrs. Quillen is in the assisted-living wing. Just go down this corridor, take a left, and then it's the third right. You'll find her apartment down that hall."

Armed with directions, they ventured deeper into the facility, their footsteps softened by the plush carpeting. As they walked, they couldn't help but notice the little alcoves outside each door—spaces where the residents could personalize their entries. Welcome signs, pumpkins, and pots of vibrant mums were popular. They even spotted an array of hand-crafted Norwegian ornaments and trinkets, courtesy of Olga Svenson.

Finally, they arrived at Ellen Quillen's door. They knocked and waited. It took a few moments, but the door eventually creaked open to reveal a petite elderly lady with snowy white hair, leaning on her walker for support. Her face lit up with a blend of curiosity and warmth.

"Hello," she greeted them, her voice rising in question at the end.

"Hi, Mrs. Quillen," Bunny began, smiling as genuinely as she felt. "I'm Bunny, this is Sam, and this is Andie. Father Frank from St. Mary's said you might be able to help us with something. May we come in?"

"Of course, of course," she said, her eyes twinkling as she stepped aside to let them enter. "Please make yourselves at home, and please call me Ellen."

Her small apartment felt like a cocoon of yester-years—photographs of younger days adorned the walls, a crocheted blanket was neatly folded on the armchair, and a delicate scent of lavender hung in the air.

The layout was simple but thoughtful—a compact kitchenette sat just to the right of the entrance, equipped with basic appliances and a small dining table set for two. The living room was the centerpiece of the apartment, featuring overstuffed furniture.

Ellen's eyes sparkled with genuine happiness at their presence. "I rarely get visitors these days. Would you like some coffee? I could put on a pot," she offered, her voice tinged with a gracious enthusiasm.

"That would be lovely, thank you," Bunny replied as Andie handed over the bag of pastries they had brought. With deft movements that belied her age, Ellen carefully unwrapped the pastries, arranged them on a fine china dish, and set it on the coffee table for her guests.

"Now then," Ellen said, settling into her armchair, "what did Father Frank think I could help you with?"

Taking this as their cue, Bunny and Sam began to recount their quest to find the intended recipient of the unopened Christmas gift and how clues had led them to her doorstep. As they unfolded the story, they produced the old church bulletin that Sam had discovered—articles and all.

As Bunny and Sam unfolded their story, Ellen's

eyes took on a faraway look, her gaze turning inward to memories long stored away. The weight of those years was palpable in her eyes. She nodded along with their recounting as if confirming details to herself, lost in a reverie of a time long past.

Setting out steaming mugs of coffee on the table beside the dish of pastries, Ellen eased herself back into her armchair and began her own tale. "My husband, God rest his soul, was killed suddenly in an accident. It was... unexpected, to say the least. We had two young children, and I was a housewife. Suddenly, there was no income, only a mountain of medical bills and the looming costs of a funeral. The church... oh, they were our saving grace. They helped us so much during that difficult time."

Her eyes moistened as she continued, "That Christmas was a bleak one, but our congregation made sure the children had gifts to open. They did their best to bring some light into a very dark time for us."

Andie, who had been listening intently, leaned forward and gently placed the beautifully wrapped gift on the table in front of Ellen. "Could this possibly be one of those gifts?" she asked, her voice tinged with cautious optimism.

Ellen looked at the gift, her eyes scanning the

AUTUMN TIDES

wrapping paper and ribbon, then shook her head slowly but decidedly. "No, I don't think so. I remember that Christmas vividly, and I'm certain there were no leftover gifts. Also, this wrapping paper doesn't look familiar to me. And 'Urchin'? I have no idea who that could be. The gifts from the congregation were all addressed to the children by name, Linda and Tom."

A pall of disappointment settled over the room. "You're sure?" Bunny asked.

Ellen nodded. "Definitely. I'm sorry."

Andie's hopes deflated. They'd been so close, and she had been sure she'd found the person who should have the gift. She sighed and took a sip of her coffee. It looked like they would have to start again from square one.

———

AFTER A HEARTWARMING HALF hour with Ellen, Bunny, Sam, and Andie left her apartment with a mixture of contentment and disappointment. As they navigated their way through the maze of hallways in Tall Pines, Sam broke the silence.

"Do you think there's a chance Ellen could be wrong about the gift? I mean, it was a long time ago."

183

Bunny shook her head. "I don't think so. Ellen seemed mentally sharp, and she was insistent that the gift wasn't from that Christmas. Plus 'Urchin' doesn't match any of her kids' names."

Andie, who had been quiet, chimed in, "I agree. I hope you two don't mind if we drop off these muffins to my mom since we're here already."

"Of course not. We'd love to see Addie," Bunny said.

The trio continued to the memory-care wing and soon found themselves at Addie's room. Addie looked up from her seat by the window. After a moment of hesitation, her eyes sparkled with faint recognition. "Oh, Bunny and Sam. It's been ages!"

"How are you, Addie?" Bunny asked.

"Fine, and you? Are you going to art school now? And Sam, you're at the police academy, aren't you?"

Bunny and Sam exchanged a glance, then both looked at Andie, who gave a subtle shrug. They decided to play along.

"Yes, we've really been hitting the books," Sam said.

"That's good."

Addie's face creased in confusion, lost somewhere in the past, so Andie decided to try to bring her back to the present. She stepped forward, holding out the chocolate chip muffins. "We brought you some muffins, Mom."

Addie took the bag but seemed momentarily distracted, her eyes drifting past them to glance into the hallway as if she were expecting someone.

"Who are you looking for?" Andie asked, following her gaze.

"Jane," Addie responded, a hint of anticipation lacing her voice.

"Jane isn't coming today. But would you like to call her?"

Addie nodded, and Andie dialed the number.

"Hey, Andie, how'd it go?" Jane knew that the three of them were coming to Tall Pines in the hopes of finding the person the gift belonged to.

Andie sighed. "No, we struck out. But we're not giving up. We're actually at Mom's room right now. She wants to talk to you."

Andie handed her phone to Addie, who eagerly took it. "Jane, sweetie, make sure you finish your homework before you go out with your friends, all right?" Addie told her.

Jane chuckled on the other end. "Don't worry, Mom. I won't go anywhere until it's done."

Andie took back the phone, laughing. "I guess that message was important to Mom."

"No doubt. Thanks for calling. I'll see you later at the big art gallery reveal tonight, right?"

"Absolutely. Can't wait!"

# CHAPTER THIRTY-ONE

As Jane hung up the phone, her smile remained. Picking up a duster, she gently swept it across the antique buffet table in the living room. It used to bother her that her mother sometimes thought it was still the past, but she had learned to roll with it. After all, her mom still knew who she was, and that was no small blessing.

She moved on to dust a side table. It hadn't been an easy decision to put Addie in Tall Pines, but it had been the right one. Addie was thriving there. Once she'd settled into Tall Pines and started her new medications, her dementia had miraculously halted its progression.

It was funny how what you thought you wanted wasn't really what you needed. Just a few years ago,

Jane had wanted nothing more than to retire. Then her mother's memory issues had escalated. Jane had resisted taking over Tides Inn, the family business. But now, she found she loved it—loved being the keeper of her family's legacy. Life's unexpected turns had led her exactly where she needed to be.

As Jane made her way into the foyer, Susan, Betty, Carol, and Margie came down the stairs.

"Oh, Jane, our stay here has been absolutely wonderful!" Susan exclaimed, her eyes twinkling with genuine happiness.

"Please extend our warmest thanks to Brenda; her breakfasts have been the highlight of our mornings," Betty chimed in.

"You're all too kind." Jane beamed. The four women had been great guests, and she wished they weren't checking out today. "If you'd like, you're welcome to extend your stay. We don't have any other bookings coming up soon. And the art gallery is having its grand opening tonight. Plus the Prelude festival is just kicking off!"

The women exchanged glances, apparently weighing their commitments against the pull of yet another evening in the idyllic town. Carol's eyes had a far-off look as she pondered. "I have my grandson's football game this weekend, and I've promised to be there. And we already dropped off the rental car so we could just uber back to the airport."

"We really should get back to our dogs." Susan glanced at Betty, who nodded.

"But that art gallery opening," Margie mused, her eyes sparkling with curiosity. "The paper they've put up on the windows has us all guessing. What a clever marketing strategy that was."

Internally, Jane chuckled. If only they knew that Maxi's "brilliant marketing move" had been born more out of desperation than strategy. But if the mystery drew people in, then who was Jane to correct their assumptions?

"Maxi does have a way of getting people talking," Jane said diplomatically, her lips curling into a sly smile. "It's going to be quite the event. But of course, I understand if you have other commitments."

The women looked at one another, the temptation clear in their eyes but reality pulling them in another direction. .

Finally, Carol said, "I guess we'll have to think about it and discuss it, so don't hold the rooms for us if you get other reservations."

"I am curious about the art gallery, though, Do you have any insider info on what the showing will actually feature?" Betty asked, her eyes twinkling with curiosity.

Jane leaned against the check-in desk, enjoying the moment of speculation. "To be honest, even I don't know what's going to be displayed. Maxi has been incredibly tight-lipped about it. It's as much a mystery to me as it is to the rest of the town."

"Oh, how intriguing!" Betty exclaimed. "What do you think it could be, Jane?"

Jane considered the possibilities. "Well, Maxi has eclectic taste. It could range from traditional landscapes to avant-garde installations. She's been so secretive, it really could be anything."

"What about a series of paintings focused on the beauty of Prelude?" suggested Margie, her eyes lighting up at the thought.

"Or maybe something provocative that challenges the norms?" Carol proposed, wiggling her eyebrows for added effect.

"I wouldn't be surprised if it's something abstract," said Susan. "You know, something that makes you tilt your head and squint, wondering what on earth you're looking at."

Betty laughed. "Or perhaps it's a mixture of all those things."

Jane nodded, entertained by their guesses. "All

very plausible. I guess we'll find out soon enough. I must admit, the suspense is part of the fun."

"Yes, we may have to delay leaving until later tonight just so we can see," Carol added, clearly more tempted than ever to stay.

Margie sighed. "Changing flights could be problematic, though."

"If you guys don't make it to the gallery, I'll let you all know what Maxi unveils tonight," Jane promised.

"Please do," they all echoed.

Betty added, "And now, we're off to walk downtown for some last-minute shopping. See you later."

# CHAPTER THIRTY-TWO

M axi meandered through the gallery, her heels clicking softly against the polished wooden floor, her phone pressed to her ear. "Chandler, you should see it—the entrance is graced by this rosemaling painting that practically dances on the canvas. And Olga's hand-carved dala horse? A masterpiece under the skylight."

The gallery setup had been completed, and Maxi and Olga had gone home to change. Now they were in the gallery alone with James, waiting to open.

Maxi adjusted the waist on her fitted emerald-green dress and glanced at Olga and James. Olga wore a navy dress that shimmered under the gallery lights, while James, in a tailored charcoal suit and crisp white shirt, looked every inch the proud husband.

"Sounds intriguing, Maxi," Chandler's voice buzzed from the other end. "You've done a spectacular job shrouding all this in mystery, what with the papered windows. Clever marketing!"

A modest smile curled Maxi's lips. "Well, sometimes, the allure is in the unknown, don't you think?" She chose not to reveal that the papered windows had been more a stroke of necessity than genius.

"I'd love to see it all. Send me some pictures, won't you?"

"Absolutely," Maxi assured him, her eyes lingering on a delicately sculpted glass figure near her. "Pictures will be on their way."

She ended the call, slipped the phone into her clutch, and turned back to James and Olga. "Chandler wants pictures."

"Oh dear, I hope he won't be disappointed." Olga pressed her palm to her face. The older woman suddenly seemed a bit overwhelmed with the idea of having a gallery showing.

"I'm sure he won't be," James assured her, handing her a bottle of water.

Maxi's eyes twinkled, but her stomach churned with a mixture of excitement and jitters. "Hopefully, everyone else will like it too. What if covering the windows has the opposite effect and no one comes?"

James laughed. "Have you looked out? Half the town is out there."

Maxi and Olga exchanged looks of panic and raced to the windows then peeked out between the gaps in the paper.

Maxi's nerves eased a bit. Faces both familiar and new were gathering. Jane and Mike, Andie and Shane, Bunny and Sam, Claire and Rob—all waiting for her moment.

Taking a deep, steadying breath, she glanced at the clock. "All right, everyone, it's showtime."

As James and Olga began tearing down the paper barriers, Maxi pushed open the door and let everyone in.

AS BUNNY STEPPED into the gallery, her disappointment about the Quillen family not being the ones the gift belonged to evaporated, overtaken by the sheer splendor of the space. She squeezed Sam's hand, stealing a glance at him. He looked remarkably handsome in a sharp, likely new charcoal-gray suit. It complemented her own lavender dress—a flattering, flowy piece that made her feel radiant.

Andie and Shane were already inside, their eyes

wandering across the artwork. Andie wore a classy sky-blue wrap dress that contrasted beautifully with her dark hair, while Shane was in a black suit with a matching green tie. Jane and Mike were not far behind. Jane sported a champagne-colored cocktail dress which gave her an air of vintage elegance. Mike looked dapper in a navy-blue suit with a light-blue shirt.

Joining them, Bunny couldn't help but beam. "Isn't this place incredible?"

"It really is," Andie agreed. "Olga has outdone herself."

"Olga's work is phenomenal," Jane chimed in, her eyes still scanning the pieces around her. "I have a couple of her smaller works at Tides. They add such character to the place."

As they chatted, Bunny felt a swell of pride. She had been the bridge that connected Maxi and Olga.

Maxi and Olga rushed over to the group, their faces glowing with joy and accomplishment. Hugs and congratulations were exchanged, laughter bubbling around them like champagne.

"You guys, this wouldn't have even happened without Bunny," Maxi declared, causing Olga to nod in agreement.

Bunny blushed. "Oh, no, I can't take credit for any of this," she demurred.

As if on cue, the room filled with a low, appreciative hum. Snippets of conversation floated toward them, phrases like "It's brilliant" and "The colors are so vibrant" weaving through the air, punctuating the atmosphere with a sense of awe and admiration. Maxi and Olga beamed, soaking in the praise.

Maxi, never one to let the spotlight shine solely on her, pivoted the conversation. "So, how is everyone? And how's your foster dog, Rob?"

"He's doing great," Rob responded, his eyes twinkling.

"We might be getting a little too attached." Claire shrugged.

"I don't see Sandee around," Maxi continued. "How's the whole Beach Bones situation?"

Claire smiled. "I may have an update, but I'll fill you guys in at our usual coffee meetup at Sandcastles. Tonight is about you and Olga. I don't want to detract from that."

Just as everyone nodded in agreement, Olga's children came rushing over. Their faces were etched with frowns, sending a ripple of unease through Bunny's stomach.

"Mom, you did all this?" Kristen's eyes widened as she took in the room, her gaze tinged with awe.

Olga smiled warmly. "I made the pieces, but Maxi arranged them into this beautiful gallery. We're a team."

Richard's brows furrowed, concern etched on his face. "But, Mom, this is a lot of work."

"Oh, it is," Olga agreed, her eyes twinkling. "But when have you ever known me to sit idle? Keeping busy keeps the mind and body young."

Finally, the tension on Kristen and Richard's faces eased into smiles. They moved in to hug their mother. "Well, you must be on to something," Kristen said, "because you're acting years younger than your age."

"We're sorry for trying to push you into assisted living," Richard added. "Clearly, you don't need it."

"Thank you." Olga looked at her children fondly. "I understand you were only looking out for my well-being, but I'm fine in the house. I still garden and rake the leaves and can take care of most everything I did years ago."

"You're right, Mom. I guess we got a little overprotective." Richard chuckled before adding, "So does this mean you're coming over to rake my lawn next week?"

Olga laughed. "Oh, don't push your luck!"

Olga's arms wrapped around Kristen and

Richard's shoulders as they moved away from the group, their path taking them toward a display featuring intricately crafted dala horses.

"Remember when Grandma Johnson used to put these in all of her windows?" Olga said, her voice tinged with nostalgia.

Kristen and Richard looked at each other then back at the dala horses, their expressions softening. "I'd forgotten about that," Kristen admitted.

Sally joined the group. Her hair wasn't in its usual braid and flowed freely past her shoulders for once, and her outfit was a colorful departure from her usual work clothes, with a red skirt and colorful top.

"Bunny, you look wonderful tonight," Sally said, her smile as bright as her skirt.

"So do you," Bunny returned the compliment.

Sally nodded toward Olga. "Looks like Olga finally got her kids to see the light."

"It seems that way," Maxi said. "I'm delighted for her."

"Me too. I hope my kids don't try to put me in a home before my time," Sally added with a wink.

Laughter rippled through the group. Everyone knew that if there was one person in town who could manage a home all on her own, it was Sally.

Sally turned to Bunny. "So how is it going with that mystery you were trying to solve?"

Bunny filled Sally in on their latest disappointment.

"Intriguing," Sally said, visibly interested. "And you found it in an old trunk? Was it a big gift?"

Andie held her hands apart, forming a small rectangle. "No, just a little box, about this big," she said, indicating a size of roughly three inches.

"And you have no clues?" Sally asked, her eyes narrowing.

"None, really." Andie sighed. "The tag just had a nickname—Urchin."

At the mention of the name, Sally's eyes widened, her posture straightening. "Urchin, you say? Now, that's a name I haven't heard in years, but I think I know who that might be. Even better, she's in town right now!"

Andie and Bunny exchanged astounded glances.

"In town? Where?" Andie stammered, hardly able to contain her surprise.

Sally nodded, her face alight with excitement. "Yes, she's right at Tides. Betty! We grew up together, and Urchin was her family's nickname for her. Jane, you must have heard me call her that when I saw them at Tides."

Jane shook her head regretfully. "I remember seeing you greet them, but with all the commotion of the day, I must've missed that." Jane's expression turned somber. "I've got some bad news. They were planning to leave tonight."

Bunny's eyes widened, her heartbeat quickening. "Tonight? What time?"

Jane looked at her watch. "They weren't sure. Actually, they did talk about extending to see the art show, but I don't see them here, so I'm afraid they decided to leave."

Bunny grabbed Andie's hand and tugged her toward the door. "We need to get to Tides. There might still be time to catch them!"

# CHAPTER THIRTY-THREE

Betty strained to drag her now-overstuffed suitcase down the stairs. "I don't know how I managed to fit everything in here!" she exclaimed, her voice tinged with both exasperation and delight.

Susan, Carol, and Margie looked up from the foyer and chuckled. "Well, it was a fruitful trip, wasn't it? The grandkids will absolutely adore the art we got for them," Carol remarked, smiling warmly at the thought.

Just then, a car screeched to a halt outside. Margie quipped, "Gosh, I hope that's not our Uber driver showing off his skills."

Peering out the window, Susan recognized Andie stepping out of the car, her face flushed and focused. Close behind her were Bunny and Sam. "Hey, that looks like Jane's sister. She seems to be in quite the rush."

Before they could speculate further, the door flew open, and in rushed Andie, followed by Bunny and Sam, their faces a mix of urgency and relief.

"Oh, I'm so glad we caught you before you left!" Bunny exclaimed, visibly relieved.

Betty felt a twinge of unease. "Is something the matter?"

"No, not really," Andie assured her. "This might seem a bit odd, but we've been looking for someone with the nickname Urchin, and Sally said that it might be you."

At the mention of the nickname, Betty's expression shifted to one of bittersweet nostalgia. "Yes, that was me. My family used to call me Urchin because I loved the sea and would always find sea urchins in the tide pools as a child. It's sad, really. You can hardly find them anymore."

The room quieted for a moment, the weight of the memory settling in. "It was a special name, but it also reminds me of my sister, Heidi. She loved the sea just as much as I did."

Bunny and Andie exchanged glances, sensing that they were on the cusp of resolving a mystery and yet uncovering new emotional depths they had not anticipated.

Andie carefully extracted the small, wrapped box from her pocket. "Then I think this is for you," she said, extending it to Betty.

Betty's eyes widened at the sight of the little package. There was something hauntingly familiar about the handwriting—she recognized it as Heidi's. "Where did you find this?" she asked, almost breathless.

Andie explained that the tiny gift had been found in a trunk she'd bought at an estate sale. "We've been trying to find its rightful owner, and it looks like we've succeeded."

The room hushed into silence as Betty contemplated the small package in her hands. "Should I open it?" she wondered aloud.

"Yes!" Susan, Carol, and Margie responded in unison, their excitement palpable.

Gently unwrapping the package, her charm bracelet jingling softly with each movement, Betty discovered a sterling silver urchin charm lying in the palm of her hand. Her eyes misted over at the sight.

It was unmistakably from Heidi, who not only had called her Urchin more than anyone else but had also contributed many of the charms that adorned her bracelet. Heidi must have bought this charm before her tragic accident and had been saving it. Somehow, it had gotten mixed in with the items that were sold off in the estate sale after they'd sold the house—during those sorrow-filled days when the family was steeped in grief.

But now, as she held the charm, Betty felt a profound sense of closure. This was the sign she had been seeking for years, a poignant, tangible connection to a past filled with love and a sister deeply missed.

"Thank you," she said softly to Bunny, Sam, and Andie. The words seemed insufficient for the emotional journey the small object had taken her on, but they were all she had. Hugs were exchanged all around, their warmth reaching deep into her soul.

Just then, an Uber pulled up outside, breaking the spell. Betty, Susan, Carol, and Margie gathered their things and headed out, waving their final goodbyes.

## CHAPTER THIRTY-FOUR

The next morning, Claire stood behind the counter at Sandcastles, ringing up a customer.

"Do you think she'll show?" Hailey asked. Claire had filled her in about inviting Sandee for a chat.

Claire shrugged. "I have no idea." Then, spotting a figure at the entrance, she added, "Oh, there she is."

Sandee walked in, a far cry from her usual immaculate appearance. She wore jeans and a sweatshirt, a few stray dog hairs clinging to the fabric. Her hair, normally perfectly styled, was pulled back into a simple ponytail. Yet her expression was one of a soft half smile, and her eyes held a light Claire had never seen before.

"Hi," Sandee said softly, her voice tinged with

vulnerability. In that moment, Claire knew she had made the right decision in inviting her.

"What would you like to eat or drink?" Claire asked as she led Sandee to a secluded table in the corner.

"Just coffee for me, thanks," Sandee replied.

They settled into their seats, the tension in the air palpable. Both women looked nervous, but as they made eye contact, it was as if an unspoken agreement passed between them.

Sandee took a deep breath, her eyes meeting Claire's. "Look, I want to clear the air right off the bat about Peter. I never stole him from you. He told me you two were separated and getting a divorce."

Claire felt as if the ground had shifted beneath her. "What? That wasn't the case at all. I had no idea he was cheating."

"Yeah, well, it turns out he's a good liar," Sandee said, a hint of bitterness touching her voice. "So, anyway, I apologize for my part in all that—and for the way I've treated you in the past."

Claire was taken aback by Sandee's candor. The tension that had been building up over the years seemed to deflate in an instant. "Thank you, Sandee. I appreciate that. I should apologize too. Tammi has always encouraged me to think more graciously of you."

At the mention of Tammi, Sandee's eyes softened, and her lips curved into a genuine smile. "Tammi's a good kid, a really nice person. You should be proud."

Claire's heart swelled, and her eyes sparkled. "I am, very proud."

For the first time, the two women felt a connection, a shared sense of understanding.

Claire took a sip of her coffee, her fingers gripping the mug a bit more tightly than usual. She still felt a tad nervous about what she was about to propose, but something about this newfound understanding with Sandee made it seem like the right time. "So, about the Beach Bones thing—"

Sandee cut her off, her expression softening. "You can use the name, Claire. I apologize for being so difficult about it earlier. It's just that I'm starting fresh, and it felt like the first thing I was truly successful at on my own."

Claire nodded, her heart buoyed by Sandee's sincerity. "Actually, that's sort of what I wanted to talk to you about. I was thinking... what about a partnership?"

"A partnership?" Sandee looked genuinely surprised, her eyes widening. "How would that work?"

Claire began outlining her vision. "We could divide up the work, collaborate on some new recipes, and sell the treats here at the bakery as well as other locations. You have a knack for sales; you could be the one to pitch our products to other shops." Claire paused and chuckled. "And, I have to ask—what on earth do you put in those red dog biscuits? Dogs seem to really love them."

Sandee laughed, her eyes twinkling. "Well, it's a secret recipe. But if we're going to be partners, I suppose I can let you in on it."

Claire felt a mixture of relief and excitement. "So you'll consider it?"

Sandee nodded, her gaze locking onto Claire's. "I'll look forward to it."

Claire's eyes met Sandee's once again, and the newfound camaraderie between them felt like a warm glow.

"So, how's Spot doing?" Sandee inquired, her tone gentle.

"Spot's doing great. Rob is getting really attached to him," Claire replied.

Sandee nodded. "We still haven't found the owners. Of course, we're doing our best to give them every chance to claim him."

"Well, if they don't, I think Spot has a home,"

Claire said, her eyes shining with a mix of happiness and slight concern.

Sandee's smile echoed Claire's sentiment, but her expression quickly shifted to a frown as she looked over Claire's shoulder. Claire turned around to see what caught her eye, and there was Peter, arm in arm with a young blond woman.

"Is that Peter with a new girlfriend?" Claire asked, a touch of disbelief in her voice.

"Yep," Sandee confirmed, her gaze still fixed on them.

Claire squinted for a better look and then turned back to Sandee. "She looks even younger than you."

Sandee craned her neck slightly for a second look and nodded. "She does, the poor thing."

Claire leaned in across the table, looking Sandee directly in the eyes. "Should we warn her?"

"Do you think she'd listen?" Sandee questioned, her brows furrowing slightly.

Claire shook her head. "Probably not."

With a knowing look, Sandee raised her coffee mug. "Let's just be glad that neither one of us is that poor girl."

Claire clinked her mug against Sandee's and grinned. "I couldn't agree with you more."

SANDEE STEPPED OUT OF SANDCASTLES, the bakery's doorbell chiming softly behind her. The air was crisp but not too cold, the sky was a vivid blue, and the last of the autumn leaves were making their graceful descent from the trees, carpeting the sidewalk in a kaleidoscope of colors. She inhaled deeply, savoring the sweet scent of baked goods still lingering in the air.

As she walked down the bustling street, Sandee's boots crunched on the fallen leaves as her thoughts replayed the meeting she'd just had with Claire. She was amazed at how well it had gone and had been pleasantly surprised by the warm atmosphere between them. The proposal of a partnership had been the furthest thing from her mind when she'd entered the bakery, but now, it felt like the beginning of something wonderful.

Claire had even extended an invitation to join her, Maxi, Jane, and Andie for coffee, but Sandee had declined, excusing herself politely. One change at a time, she thought. One relationship mended, one step forward. There was a slight pang of regret, but she assured herself that there'd be other opportunities.

As she approached the storefront of a quirky little antiques shop, she spotted a dog tethered to a lamp-post. She couldn't resist. Bending down, she petted the dog's soft fur. Its tail wagged in response, and for a brief moment, she felt a simple, unconditional love that only animals seemed to offer.

Standing, she continued her walk toward the animal rescue shelter, at which she was volunteering. Cleaning out litter boxes wasn't glamorous work, but it was honest and it was needed. And strangely enough, she found satisfaction in it. Gone were the days when her self-worth was measured by the number of social events she attended or the brands she wore. Now, she found meaning in contributing to a cause greater than herself—in providing comfort to animals who had none.

As she neared the shelter, Sandee couldn't help but feel proud of the person she was becoming. The old Sandee, the insecure mean girl who'd trample over anyone to get what she wanted, was becoming a distant memory. Every step she took felt like a step away from that past and toward a future that held so much promise, so much more substance.

After entering the shelter, she took off her coat and rolled up her sleeves. There was work to be done, but for the first time in a long time, Sandee was genuinely excited about doing it. And as she set about her tasks, each small action felt like a piece of a new identity falling into place—one built on empathy, compassion, and authentic connections.

## CHAPTER THIRTY-FIVE

Claire was cleaning off the table when Jane walked into Sandcastles, her eyes scanning the bakery before landing on Claire. "Was that Sandee I saw leaving?" Jane inquired, setting her purse down on the counter.

Claire's smile widened. "Yep, that was her."

Jane glanced back out the window toward the sunlit street Sandee had just walked down. "She looked... happy."

"You know," Claire began, pausing to tuck a stray hair behind her ear, "I think she was."

Jane raised an eyebrow, intrigued. "So what happened?"

Claire chuckled. "I'll spill all the tea once everyone

gets here. But since you're early, you're on table-setting duty."

Jane laughed and nodded, accepting her assignment as Claire moved to the display case. She selected an assortment of freshly baked pastries, including a chocolate cruller that Jane requested. Claire arranged the pastries on a serving tray while Jane made the coffees just the way everyone liked them.

They had just set everything on the table when Maxi and Andie arrived.

"What perfect timing we have," Andie said as she sat down in front of the black coffee and slid a danish onto her plate.

Everyone else settled into their seats and grabbed a pastry. The conversation naturally turned to Maxi's gallery show.

"I think it was a smashing success, even if I do say so myself." Maxi beamed. "We had record attendance, and Olga sold several pieces."

Claire clapped her hands, delighted. "Oh, that's wonderful! And what did Chandler think?"

"I sent him a video, and let's just say he was more than impressed." Maxi grinned. "But the real win was Olga's kids finally coming around, realizing she's perfectly capable of living in her own home. That alone made the night for me."

Everyone nodded, sharing in Maxi's joy.

"But enough about me." Maxi then turned her attention to Andie. "What was that big emergency last night? You, Bunny, and Sam rushed out of here like the place was on fire!"

Andie leaned back, her face glowing with the satisfaction of a mystery solved. "Well, it turns out that the gift was meant for Betty, who was staying at Tides. You won't believe how it all came together. Even after Bunny and Sam put in hours of research, all it took was Sally recognizing the name on the gift as Betty's nickname."

"So you rushed off to Tides in the hopes of catching her?" Maxi asked.

"Yes. Jane said they were leaving last night, so we were hoping to catch them before they left," Andie said.

"And did you?" Maxi asked, her eyes wide with curiosity.

"Yes. They were practically on their way out the door!" Andie said.

"Did you give her the gift?" Claire cut a carrot muffin in half and put one side on her plate.

"I did." Andie smiled. "It was a sterling silver urchin charm. You should have seen her face when she opened it. Turns out, the charm was from her late sister, Heidi."

Jane nodded, "Ah, yes, Betty had mentioned her sister to me and how she'd been looking for some sort of connection, a sign, maybe."

"Then I bet the charm was the connection she was looking for," Andie mused.

Jane nodded. "I'm happy for her. They were nice ladies. They even left a wonderful note at the reception desk. Looks like we'll be seeing them next year!"

"That's great to hear," Claire chimed in. "Sounds like everything worked out nearly perfectly."

Andie grinned. "It did. Although Bunny was a bit disappointed that we didn't actually solve the mystery through hard-boiled detective work, both she and Sam were thrilled to have played a part in reuniting Betty with such a sentimental treasure."

Jane, shifting her attention from Andie's delightful tale, turned to Claire. "So, spill the beans! I saw Sandee leaving Sandcastles as I walked in. What happened?"

Claire took a deep breath, her face glowing with an air of hope and new beginnings. "Well, Sandee and I are going to work on a project together. We're considering a partnership for Beach Bones!"

The table went silent for a moment, a mixture of

surprise and curiosity painted on everyone's faces. Maxi broke the silence first. "A partnership? With Sandee? Wow, that's unexpected!"

Claire nodded. "It is. But you know, I think we may have misjudged her. She's changed, really changed. Did you know she drove all the way down to New York to rescue dogs affected by the flooding? Risked her own safety for it."

Jane looked impressed. "That does sound like the action of a changed person."

Claire continued, "She was fooled by Peter, just like I was. I think it's high time we gave her another chance, and honestly, I'm looking forward to working with her."

Andie raised her coffee mug in the air. "Well, here's to new beginnings!"

Everyone clinked their mugs together, the sound echoing the harmony and unity that filled the room.

Claire looked around the table at her friends, grateful for the love and community that seemed to wrap itself around every corner of their small town. "You know, it really does seem like everything always works out in the end."

ALSO BY MEREDITH SUMMERS

**Lobster Bay Series:**

*Saving Sandcastles (Book 1)*

*Changing Tides (Book 2)*

*Making Waves (Book 3)*

*Shifting Sands (Book 4)*

*Seaside Bonds (Book 5)*

*Seaside Bookclub (Book 6)*

*Autumn Tides (Book 7)*

**Shell Cove Series:**

*Beachcomber Motel (Book 1)*

*Starfish Cottage (Book 2)*

*Saltwater Sweets (book 3)*

**Pinecone Falls Christmas Series:**

*Christmas at Cozy Holly Inn (Book 1)*

*Cozy Hometown Christmas (Book 2)*

*Grumpy Cozy Christmas (Book 3)*

———————————————

**Meredith Summers / Annie Dobbs**

**Firefly Inn Series:**

Another Chance (Book 1)

Another Wish (Book 2)

-------

# ABOUT THE AUTHOR

Meredith Summers writes cozy mysteries as USA Today Bestselling author Leighann Dobbs and crime fiction as L. A. Dobbs.

She spent her childhood summers in Ogunquit Maine and never forgot the soft soothing feeling of the beach. She hopes to share that feeling with you through her books which are all light, feel-good reads.

Join her newsletter for sneak peeks of the latest books and release day notifications:

https://lobsterbay1.gr8.com

This is a work of fiction.

None of it is real. All names, places, and events are products of the author's imagination. Any resemblance to real names, places, or events are purely coincidental, and should not be construed as being real.

AUTUMN TIDES

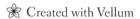 Created with Vellum